THE BIG GIRL
AND OTHER STORIES

by
ALAGU SUBRAMANIAM

Every effort has been made to trace copyright holders and
to obtain their permission for the use of copyright material.
The publisher would be grateful to be notified of any omissions.

Published by the Bay Owl Press, 2018
an imprint of the Perera-Hussein Publishing House
www.pererahussein.com

ISBN: 978-955-1723-41-5

All Rights Reserved. No part of this publication may be reproduced, stored in a retrieval system or transmitted in any form by any means, electrical, mechanical, photocopying, recording or otherwise, without prior written permission of the publishers and copyright holders.

The moral rights of the author have been asserted.

Copyright © ALAGU SUBRAMANIAM

The Big Girl and Other Stories is a collection of fictional short stories,
first published by the Author in February 1964
with Universal Printers Limited, Ratmalana

The Author expresses his grateful thanks to
EARLE WICKRAMASINGHE for his helpful suggestions
and generous encouragement.

Printed and bound in Sri Lanka by Samayawardhana Printers

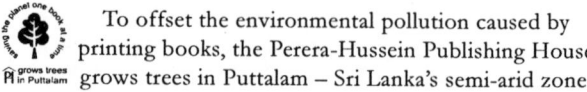 To offset the environmental pollution caused by printing books, the Perera-Hussein Publishing House grows trees in Puttalam – Sri Lanka's semi-arid zone.

THE BIG GIRL
AND OTHER STORIES

by
ALAGU SUBRAMANIAM

COLOMBO

ABOUT THIS BOOK

ALL the stories in this book have been previously published in anthologies, periodicals, magazines and newspapers in various parts of the world. Many of them have made more than one appearance. Some were broadcast in the Home and Overseas Services of the B.B.C.

THE MATHEMATICIAN achieved some distinction in a German translation of the story which was included in a volume published in Heidelberg entitled KURZ ERZAEHLT: DIE SCHOENSTEN GESCHICHTEN DER WELTLITERATUR (Briefly Told: The Finest Stories, in World Literature).

THE BIG GIRL, was rendered into Russian and Polish. These and other stories have also been translated into the Tamil and Kannada languages. A Sinhala version of this book is in preparation.

❊ ❊ ❊

"THE story called 'The Mathematician', by Alagu Subramaniam has the flavour of Chekhov's good-humoured raillery."
- Sean O' Faolâin in THE LISTENER (London).

❈ ❈ ❈

"THE THORN by Alagu Subramaniam is an admirable story. Here man's normal voice tells a moving tale of childhood innocence and 'authoritarian stupidity'
- J. Maclaren-Ross in THE TRIBUNE (London).

❈ ❈ ❈

"SUBRAMANIAM contributes interesting work."
- Walter Allen in TIME AND TIDE (London).

❈ ❈ ❈

"EXTREMELY interesting stories."
- A. S. Raman: Editor, ILLUSTRATED WEEKLY OF INDIA.

ALAGU SUBRAMANIAM is a Ceylon-born writer, a Barrister-at-Law of the Honourable Society of Lincoln's Inn and an Advocate of the Supreme Court of Ceylon. He was fortunate in his long residence in England. It was a voluntary exile coupled with an intellectual journey. He was a prominent figure in London literary circles and a spectacular personality at artists' gatherings, although he says of himself that he spent most of his time in the largest City in the world "reading, writing, walking and imagining". He was co-editor of INDIAN WRITING, a quarterly journal published in England, and was Secretary of the London Branch of Indian Progressive Writers' Association. His forthcoming books include CLOSING TIME - stories dealing with contemporary English life, and MR. MOON, a short novel with a Bloomsbury setting. His father was a judge in Ceylon, his grandfather was a literary personage and Alagu Subrarnaniam after his return to the Island has combined the dual professions of barrister and writer. He is married to a graduate teacher.

❊ ❊ ❊

"Alagu Subramaniam is a gifted writer"
— HUBERT NICHOLSON in
Half my Days and Nights.

"Mr. Subramaniam's stories earned considerable praise from literary critics during his long sojourn in London".
— C. R. MANDY in The Illustrated Weekly of India.

THE AUTHOR

CONTENTS

THE MATHEMATICIAN 15

THE CAT 26

THE THORN 32

THE CONVERT 39

THE MARKET SQUARE 51

THE FLOOD 67

THE FAN 72

PROFESSIONAL MOURNERS 78

COUSIN THAMPOO 86

THE BIG GIRL 92

DANGER 106

THE MALAYAN PENSIONER 111

THE INTERPRETER 117

TENNIS 122

THE SCHOLAR 128

SOLOMON'S JUSTICE 142

LOVELY DAY 147

FOREWORD

Reprinting of this book is for those Sri Lankan Tamils who have migrated and have fond memories of home.

When re-reading it 27 years after migrating from Sri Lanka to Australia, Alagu Subramaniam's perception of Jaffna makes me appreciate its way of life, the people and their prejudices. 'The Market Square' in particular, takes one right back to a market in Jaffna. 'Professional Mourners' is a story based on my great-grandmother's funeral, depicting the caste system, written with humour. When Alagu writes about fanning himself under a Margosa tree, you can feel the gentle breeze of the Northern province. Those of us living through cold winters will be amused at how the author's mother wraps him in woollen socks and monkey cap for the Jaffna 'pani' or cooler air during the monsoon!

It is 54 years since the first publication of this book and 48 years since the unfortunate death, aged 56, of this talented author. So much has changed in the lives of the Jaffna people, yet so little has changed.

Reason for reprinting is to bring these stories back into circulation so readers can enjoy them and they are not lost in time. This is a tribute to Alagu Subramaniam, a gifted writer who was also a barrister and whom I am proud to call my grand uncle

Premila Thurairatnam
2018

To
my brother
D. K.

THE MATHEMATICIAN

IT was a moonlit night and the people of the town were walking leisurely on the *maidan*. Among them were a newly-married couple. They did not walk abreast. The man was half a step in front of his wife. Strictly-speaking, she should have been at least a step behind her husband, but they were educated and comparatively modern. Hence half a step, which to them was a negligible distance.

Chandram, the husband, taught mathematics to senior students in a high school. His qualifications fitted him to be a lecturer in a university. That was his ambition.

Suddenly Subhadra, his wife, became thoughtful, as if she had recollected a significant event.

"What are you thinking?" asked Chandram.

"I am thinking of the days I spent at the Tamarind School. Look, look there. Do you see the building that rises above those walls?"

"Yes."

"That was where I studied."

"Oh yes, I remember now. The go-between told my parents that you were an educated girl. Did you study a lot?"

"Well, I went up to the third form. It was once my ambition to pass the Junior Cambridge examination, but I married you in the meantime."

"Are you disappointed?"

"No, oh no!" she laughed, baring her teeth to the moonlight.

"Did you study mathematics also, Pearly Teeth?"

"Yes, I did algebra and geometry."

"Well," said Chandram, "define parallel lines."

"Parallel lines are those that do not meet however far they are produced."

"That's not quite correct. Your definition is all right for one who knows only elementary mathematics."

"How would you define them?"

"Parallel lines are those that meet at infinity," said Chandram solemnly. "You see Subadhra, I am a higher mathematician."

"You are an educated man," commented his wife.

"You are educated too," replied Chandram, "but not too much. Excessive education does not befit a woman.

You are educated enough to be impressed with my learning, and you are not so educated that you get on my nerves."

Subhadra smiled, again showing her teeth which were whiter than the moonlight. Chandram, pleased with himself, wanted to go home. He led the way. His wife accompanied him, half a step behind.

❄ ❄ ❄

During the years that followed Chandram showed more interest in mathematics than in his wife. She resented it, but never expressed her resentment either in words or deeds. She bore it all like a model wife. Of course, the husband did not entirely fail in his matrimonial obligations. Subhadra gave birth to children at regular intervals.

Chandram persuaded his wife to believe that he was a genius. His was no ordinary brain, he was different from the others. The poet is devoted to his poetry and the musician to his music. They may be failures as ordinary human beings, but you have to judge them in relation to their work. Chandram should be judged in the field of mathematics and not in the social world of ordinary men. He often went for long walks, and when his wife asked him if he had met any of his friends, be would reply, 'No, I have been roaming in the realm of mathematics.' He quarrelled with his neighbours, he found fault with his servants; he solved the most difficult problems in calculus, but made mistakes in totalling tradesmen's bills. He neglected his children.

The husband and wife discussed Chandram the genius. One day he will be a Newton, at least a Ramanujam. Subhadra boasted about her husband to her friends and requested them to overlook his faults. She simplified life for him by attending to all his needs and never allowed her children to disturb their father in his work. Chandram acted like an extraordinary man. He inadvertently wore socks that didn't match, invited friends to his house but was out at the appointed time, and went for long walks in heavy rain. Chandram worked hard, his mind always on the alert for original solutions of problems. He discovered new and quicker methods and advised his students not to be frightened by verbosity in a test paper, but to ponder the question deeply and try and render the puzzle in terms of pure geometry.

But Chandram's attitude to life was not destined to go unchallenged. By winning an international prize for mathematics, he became famous and was appointed a professor at the Colombo University. The varied life of the university was not a suitable field for the new professor's idiosyncrasies. Besides, the members of the staff, in addition to their own curriculum, took an interest in other activities. Colombo itself was very different from Jaffna, the home town of Professor Chandram. Life was more complex in the city and people knew less of each other's private lives.

Chandram was jealous of his colleagues. There was Professor Sunderam, who, in addition to lecturing in history, considered himself an authority on music. He presided at most concerts. The assistant lecturer in mathematics held discourses on philosophy, while Prof. Mangalam the lecturer in philosophy, was considered a writer. Apart from the adulation he received from his students and the residents of the town for his literary work, Prof. Mangalam thought and spoke a lot about himself.

But Professor Chandram could not even indulge in self-praise successfully. In his home town he had roamed in the realm of mathematics, but in the metropolis there were so many who were roaming in the land of figures that it ceased to be original. The people who mattered were those who came out of their shells and entered the arena of life, in art or in politics. Chandram wished to be recognised in the university and given his due place, but as the years went by the staff of the university began to treat him more lightly. Chandram found that he was never asked to be the chairman of any committee, or warden of a hostel, or to act as registrar or principal of the college.

His colleagues held that they were not being unfair to Chandram. They, of course, recognised his capabilities - but only as a very clever mathematician. They were prepared to look up to Chandram with awe and respect on his discovering a new theorem like the Binomial and thus making good his claims to genius; or they gave him the alternative of widening his interests and impressing on his colleagues that he was not merely a mathematical apparatus like the slide-rule.

During the next few years Chandram became very restless. He was yearning to discover something new but discovery was by no means easy. "My predecessors have discovered everything that is to be discovered, perhaps there is nothing new," he remarked to one of his friends.

"While you are differentiating equations on the blackboard, the world is marching past you," his friend commented. "Why don't you take an interest in life? Then people will think you are somebody. As it is you are nobody."

"Don't say that. Don't say that!" shouted Chandram. "I am a genius. Do you realise that? I am a genius." He stared at his friend angrily, then controlled himself and added, "Maybe you are right. I, too, feel a pull in two directions; mathematics and the wide world; still the force of mathematics is stronger!"

The professor of mathematics, unlike the other members of the staff, did not hold himself aloof from his students. He was rather free with the undergraduates. Sometimes he even made jokes at himself or his dozen children. One day, when it rained heavily and the water began to leak through the tiles, Chandram said: "In the honours class there are only a few students, I could ask them to come home, but with you intermediate students who number a hundred I can't possibly do that, because I already have an intermediate class at home." In the course of a lecture on Permutations and Combinations he would ask: "In how many different ways is it possible to take two of my boys and two of my girls across the stream?"

The undergraduates and post-graduates naturally did not keep themselves aloof. They joined their professor in the fun. Some became too free and easy with him, others even overstepped the limit.

Chandram gave his students an excellent training in mathematics. He held tests frequently and he chose lunar days for them so that while walking in the moonlight he might meditate on some of the original solutions of his students. At one of those tests Chandram himself was present, though usually he asked his assistants to preside. Chandram was fantastically dressed and had forgotten to comb his hair. He looked like an eccentric musician.

During the test he passed up and down the room supervising. He noticed that every student was hard at work, except one whose paper seemed blank. You cannot bluff in mathematics. You either solve the problems or walk out of the hall.

Chandram also noticed that every time he looked at the student he seemed frightened, like a startled deer. The professor went near the pupil, whose paper was blank except for two lines. Even these the undergraduate covered with his palm as the professor approached him. Chandram forcibly pushed the student's hand away. The top line was now visible and it read as follows:-

Prof. Chandram plus Mathematics equals Infinity.

Chandram smiled happily, then began to pace up and down the room again. Soon after he mounted the platform and strutted about like a peacock. He was pleased with himself. "Newton, Ramanujam, Chandram. Chandram, Newton, Ramanujam," he repeated the names.

A sudden thought flashed across his mind as he descended the platform. He asked the student to show him the second line. The latter turned pale and folded his book. Chandram told him it was improper to do that and ordered him to hand over the file. The professor read;-

Prof. Chandram minus Mathematics equals Zero.

Chandram's face fell. It was such an unexpected blow that Chandram could not even regain enough composure to scold the student. He walked about like a man who had lost all his possessions. He felt like a paralytic in a room full of energetic and vital people. The University of the metropolis had reduced him to this state.

The light from the full moon spread itself like a white sheet over the *maidan* adjoining the university. People were not heavily dressed as during the day. Light shawls were carelessly thrown over the bare shoulders of men and translucent muslins held the soft contours of their wives. Subhadra, standing half a step behind her husband, loosened her jacket and let the air wander over her breasts, when she was suddenly called by her husband.

"Where are you?" he cried.

"I am just behind you."

"What is Professor Chandram plus mathematics?"

Subhadra was taken aback. She was not familiar with the term 'infinity'. Her knowledge of mathematics did not go so far. But she knew that mathematics together with her husband was something immeasurable. Subhadra used her own method of description.

"Well," she replied, "it is something greater than this world or the oceans." "Splendid," said Chandram, "your description is wonderful." He looked at her affectionately and fondled her. Subhadra, having been taught that a woman should maintain strict modesty in public, even with her husband, resisted.

"I was not doing anything," said Chandram defensively, "I was only testing the quality of the muslin." He gave his wife a sly look.

"My husband is behaving strangely today," Subhadra thought.

"No, no, oh no!" she immediately corrected herself; "he is a genius, that's why ..."

"Subhadra!"

"Yes, Professor?"

"Now, tell me, what is Professor Chandram minus mathematics?"

"That's easy," commented his wife, as her lips curled with a smile. "Well, my dear Professor, you are nothing without mathematics." Subhadra expected her husband to be delighted with her reply and to express his appreciation of her muslin dress.

She was surprised to find him reacting differently. Chandram abused his wife, threw his hands in the air and became hysterical.

A small crowd soon collected round the professor. They all looked like shadows in the moonlight. Some said that Chandram had actually gone mad, others that it was only a temporary aberration of the mind which now and again afflicts talented people, while the rest believed that he was performing the cosmic dance of Siva.

Some friends of Subhadra took her in their charge. Chandram broke through the crowd, ran to the Principal of the college, and demanded replies to his two questions. The demand was accompanied by mythological gestures, The Principal had no answer to give, became speechless, and was genuinely frightened. His wife began to scream. Her husband retained enough composure to send for the servant and ask him to call a taxi. They experienced great difficulty in removing Chandram. The servant finally overpowered the professor and put him in the taxi. While the servant held Chandram to his seat, the Principal got in and instructed the driver to take them to the Mental Hospital. Through the windows and in the moonlight he saw his wife being led home by a group of women. Chandram shouted for his wife. "You can't see her now," said the Principal in a commanding tone.

"All right," replied the professor. "It doesn't matter, I'll meet her at infinity."

A cloud covered the moon. The road no longer looked like a white sheet. Chandram became more violent and despite the darkness the driver drove furiously to the Mental Hospital.

THE CAT

"HAVE you ever been in love with a cat?" he asked me.

"No," I said. "I actually hate cats. What will you have? Ice-cream or milk-shake?"

"I'll have a glass of milk," he replied. "My cat adores milk. We have the same tastes."

He took a long sip of milk, then smacked his lips. "I know it's bad manners to smack one's lips, but my cat does. We have the same habits. It's wonderful to share one's life with a partner who has the same tastes and manners."

"What do you mean, 'partner'?" I asked curiously.

"My cat," he answered. "She's my partner. I picked her up in a London hospital, fell for her the moment I saw her- collapsed like a house of cards."

I looked straight into my friend's eyes. There was not the slightest flicker of amusement. He was in dead earnest.

"My cat is quite uncommon," he continued. "Her hair is long and curls at hairpin bends. It's crinkly and crispy like the hair of a girl from Jamaica."

This was my first encounter with my friend after many years. We had been class-mates together, but soon after finishing school he had left for England. He had spent several winters there and had acquired one kind of reputation and another. The mildest of these was that he was a good conversationalist. However, I was somewhat disappointed. I was eager to hear him discourse about his experiences in England, but he persisted in talking about his cat. I gave him full scope.

"My cat is marvellously attractive," he said. "She has sharp teeth, tilted upwards but not protruding. Don't you think it attractive?" he said. "I do. Tilted teeth excite me like a retroussé nose in a girl."

Actually, I am repelled by protruding teeth. But to be fair by my friend, I must admit that I have never given a moment's thought to tilted teeth that do not project outwards, or to turned-up noses. These were new items for me in the repertoire of a woman's glamour.

"My cat is of a rare type," he commented. "She has a long straight back and walks as if she had swallowed a foot rule."

I could not repress my laughter at his description. I now realised that he fully deserved his reputation for brilliant conversation. I suddenly became interested in his cat and, in order to keep him longer with me, I ordered some meat rolls.

"Not for me," he said, waving aside the meat dish. "I'd rather have fish-cakes. My cat adores them and I take the cue in all matters from her." I ordered fish rissoles for my guest and a plate of Vienna steak for myself. He bent down and almost kissed the rissoles when they arrived.

"The fish dish I like best is the Tamil soup," he informed me. "I don't mean mulligatawny but the richer kind. The one that contains fish, tiny crabs, prawns, jack seeds and what not. I believe it is called *kool*. Yes, *kool*. It's the best soup on the world's menu. It certainly is the king of soups. It's far more satisfying than either the Chinese noodle soup or the Italian minestrone. Whenever I have it specially prepared by Kanmani, our maid, my cat and I sit out in the garden to relish it. She cuddles herself into a cosy corner in my lap and we both eat kool out of one and the same Chinese bowl."

I now felt that I had had enough of the cat, although I was not in the least bored. In fact, I was interested so far, but I wanted my friend to take up another theme.

"Haven't you ever been in love with a woman?" I asked him.

"I have," he admitted, "many a time."

"This too will pass like the others." I made the logical inference.

"Not this one," he assured me. "Never. Those whom God hath joined together let no man put asunder ... I'm married to my cat."

"Does it know about your past affairs?" I made a frontal attack.

"Certainly, but she's catty about them all. My cat is a real woman."

"Miaow!" I cried.

"Miaow!" he echoed.

Once again I became eager to hear about my friend's activities in England.

"Tell me," I asked. "Why do you prefer to live in England?"

"The four seasons and a cat," he answered briskly.

"What do you mean?"

"Spring, summer, autumn, winter and a cat."

"What's wonderful about them and where does the cat come in?"

"You'll see. Take the spring, for instance- love and all that."

I cut him short. "I know all about love. Proceed to the others."

"In the summer you can watch cricket."

"You can do that here too," I retorted, "in brighter sunshine and for a longer season."

"But it's not the same," he informed me.

"That's all right." I gave in. "I'm not interested in cricket anyway. Well, what happens in the autumn?"

"The leaves turn yellow matching the colour of a blonde's hair. Haven't you heard the expression, 'The autumn-leaf yellow of her hair'?"

I now waited for the finale. I was convinced my companion would never be able to boost the English winter.

"What about the English winter? I hear it's terrible."

"Rubbish," he contradicted me. "In the winter an old man sits beside an old woman facing a blazing fire, and a cat cuddles cosily on the rug. There's love between the old couple. Warmth from the fire and friendship from the cat. Love, warmth and friendship. What more do you want in life?"

I began to ponder. My friend got up.

"I must really go now," he said. "My wife will be waiting for me."

"Which wife?" I asked irritably.

"Cat," he answered calmly. "You see, I met my wife at St. George's Hospital, in London, where she was a medical student. We fell in love with each other. After a fortnight's courtship we got married, and my wife Catlin, brought her pet, a huge black cat, along with her on our honeymoon, and on the very first night Catlin miaowed, purred and cuddled exactly like her pet which shared our bed. That's why I have named my wife Cat. Good night!"

THE THORN

THE matron led Parvati to her room. The girl looked round and was surprised to find the room furnished like the lady principal's. Perhaps in this town everybody lived like the English. Maybe when she grew up, she too, would live like them.

The matron asked the new pupil about life in her village. Parvati told her about her parents, Subbu, the carter and his grass-seller. She didn't know the name of the grass-seller. All she knew was that she was called Subbu's grass-seller. Why she was called that, Parvati didn't know. She only knew that he often teased her and pinched her bottom. When anybody else pinched her that way she was very angry, but when Subbu did it she was happy.

"You'll have to learn English," the matron said, "I'll give you a lesson every day."

The matron took great pains. Parvati stumbled over the alphabet. The woman grew impatient and scolded her. The girl began to cry. "Don't cry, please don't cry," said the matron, "you may find it difficult in the beginning, but soon you'll master the new alphabet. You're a clever girl and you know your arithmetic quite well."

Parvati wiped her tears with her hand. The matron brought a piece of chocolate and gave it to her. She took it, put it in her mouth and looked at the woman.

"Eat it," said the matron. "But before that you should thank me. When people give you something always say 'Thank you'."

"Thank you."

"No. You should say, 'Thank you, matron akka'."

"Thank you, matron akka."

"Have you seen this?" the matron asked, showing Parvati a picture of Jesus surrounded by little children.

"No," said Parvati. "Who is it?"

"It's a picture of Jesus, our Lord and Saviour."

"What does that mean?"

"He came to save us sinners. He died on the Cross that we might be saved." She looked at Parvati. The child was staring at the picture vacantly.

"You won't understand that now. Wait till you grow up. But let me tell you. Jesus loves little children. He said, 'Of such is the Kingdom of God.'" The girl scratched her head.

"You must go to Him, Parvati. You must. He will receive you."

"How can I go to him when I haven't even seen him? Does he come to the school?"

"Oh, you're silly," said the matron, "you don't understand anything. A Christian child would have known all this. Your parents haven't brought you up properly."

"Matron akka?"

"What is it?"

"Where are his wives?"

"Whose?" asked the matron angrily.

"His," said Parvati, pointing at the picture, "I don't know his name."

"Blasphemy!" cried the matron, placing the picture on the table and beating her head with her hands. "How dare you ask such a question? Oh, what can I do now? You have committed a sin against God."

The matron was very nervous. She believed that the child by her stupid question had committed a sin. How could she? How could she attribute a wife to Jesus, the Holiest of Holy Beings? She knelt before the picture, joined her hands and mumbled a prayer.

Parvati, who was perplexed at the behaviour of the woman, went up to her, knelt down, placed her hands in the woman's lap, and asked her forgiveness.

"I don't know how I have offended you, matron akka," she said. "I asked you if your god had two wives because our god has two."

"Who is that?"

"Subramanya."

"Oh," shouted the matron, wringing her hands, "how can you compare Jesus with your god?" She pushed the girl away.

"Go," she said, "go and sit there." Then she paced the room. She was restless. After a while she went up to the girl, stroked her hair and said, "You mustn't say such things, child. You'll learn better by and by. You must go to Jesus. He is the only One who can save you."

"But mother asked me to pray to Subramanya. She said I should repeat his name every day, and she also said I should not bow to your god."

"Listen," said the matron, placing Parvati in her lap, "you are now with us, not with your mother, and you should listen to us. If you want to be saved you must go to Jesus."

"What does it mean to be saved?"

"If you want to go to Heaven you must go to Jesus."

"Then won't mother go to heaven?" asked the girl, opening her eyes wide.

"I don't know about that," replied the matron indifferently. Then, as she saw the look of alarm in the child's eyes, she said, "I think your mother'll be all right. You see, Parvati, your mother hasn't heard of Jesus and His teachings, but those who have heard of Him and haven't answered the call will not go to Heaven."

The girl bit her finger and began to think. The matron wondered if Parvati had understood her.

They heard the school bell ring and the matron informed the new pupil that it was the afternoon recess. The day scholars would be going home for their meals while the boarders would lunch in the school.

"I'm hungry, matron akka," said Parvati, "can I have something to eat?"

"Say 'Please, matron akka'."

"Please, matron akka."

"I'll go and bring you some food," said the matron. "You can't go to the dining hall until I have taught you how to use a fork and spoon."

"What is that?"

"You'll see."

The matron soon returned with a plate of rice and curry. A fork and spoon lay thrust into the rice. Parvati stared hard.

"Don't stare, you fool," said the woman, "come here and sit by my side and let me teach you how to use these."

"No, no, I don't want to use those. I've always eaten with my fingers. Please let me eat with my fingers. I'm hungry, matron akka."

"You ate with your hands in your home. Remember, you are now in an English school. You must learn to eat the way the English eat."

"No, no, I'm afraid to touch them. That thorn might prick my hands. Please let me eat with my hands. I'm hungry, matron akka."

"Don't be foolish. This is not a thorn. It's a fork and it won't prick you. I can't allow you to eat with your hands. It is against the rules of the Tamarind School to let a new pupil go without teaching her proper manners. Now, come and sit by my side like a good girl and I'll show you how to use these."

Parvati sat by the woman's side and watched intently. The matron gave a demonstration and then the girl made an attempt at the new way of eating. Parvati held the fork as a murderer would hold a clasp knife. The matron corrected her and quite an appreciable time was spent in learning the art.

"Tell me, matron akka," said Parvati, "have I always got to use the thorn, and do all the girls in the boarding school eat with the thorn?"

"Yes."

"They must be hungry even after eating."

"Ha, ha," laughed the matron, "you're a funny girl."

"Matron akka?"

"Yes."

"Will I be saved?"

"If you go to Jesus."

"Does He also eat with the thorn?"

The matron did not answer. She got up, cleared the mess that Parvati had made with the fork and spoon, and then walked up and down the room. She was deep in thought, her eyes were riveted to the ground, and her hands fell crosswise on her buttocks. It was such a pity that the child was not a Christian, she reflected. Perhaps she could try and convert her. The Mission would be very pleased.

She turned to Parvati. The girl was yawning.

"You're tired, Parvati. I think you'd better sleep for a while."

"Ah," replied Parvati, her eyelids drooping, "ah, the thorn." And she gently stretched her body on the matron's bed and went to sleep.

THE CONVERT

"LEAVE the Christians," said a young, dark-skinned blacksmith, his plate of rice resting on the upturned palm of his left hand, his right hand lifting the food to his mouth. He looked angrily at his brother Rangu, waiting for him to speak.

The brothers were having the first meal of the day with their cousins. They sat a few yards from each other, on whatever they could get hold of in the shed which served as the smithy.

"Leave the Christians," re-echoed the cousins.

Rangu did not answer. He looked at them and then turned his gaze into the distance, his expression changing from sorrow to aloofness.

Rangu had more than once been faced with this request from his relations. At such times he felt uncomfortable.

For reasons of his own, Rangu, just after completing his education at a mission school, had been converted to Christianity. His brothers had never been to school, for their father could not afford it. But it had so happened that one day, after an open-air meeting in the market place on the outskirts of Jaffna, the manager of the mission school, who conducted the service, was so impressed by the intelligent questions of a small, shabby boy, that he had strongly recommended him for admission as a free scholar in the school. The boy was Rangu.

His parents were happy. They hoped that one day he would be able to read and write English and work in an office, instead of hammering away in the smithy.

It did not take Rangu long to become interested in his studies, and he made rapid progress. Before he went to school Rangu had helped his father, doing odd jobs for him in the smithy, and had thereby acquired a sound and healthy physique. This was helpful to him in the playground.

The new pupil soon became the favourite of both his class master and the sports master. The former was a convert and was more Christian than those who had converted him. He looked upon Rangu as a future addition to the fold.

The first lesson in every class was 'Religious Knowledge'. The students were taught stories from the Old Testament, and then the Gospels. Rangu learned these with curiosity and interest.

The missionaries were kind to him and gave their new student beautiful booklets containing religious stories told in the language of children, and also presented him with coloured shawls and white dhoties.

Rangu grew up under the guidance of his teacher, and when he reached the eighth standard he had acquired not only an elementary knowledge in the general subjects but could also recite passages from the Bible. At the annual prize-giving of the school he was awarded a prize for Religious Knowledge. The Principal remarked that it was remarkable for a non-Christian to win such a prize, and congratulated the teaching staff on their efficiency and Rangu on his intelligence.

Rangu was proud of his knowledge and often tried to show off to his parents, and especially to his brothers and cousins. He knew that it was useless to talk to them about mathematics or history, as they were illiterate. So, thinking that stories would interest even the uneducated, he unwittingly related to them tales from the Bible.

His people became suspicious. They feared that their beloved son was going the wrong way and might one day become a Christian. They had only wished him to acquire as much knowledge as would enable him to obtain a respectable position. They had often advised him to ignore the religion of his masters. They felt they were now in a muddle. They would rather have had him illiterate and working in the smithy, than a Christian, although accompanied by a salaried job.

"You mad and disloyal son!" his father had once abused him, when Rangu admitted that he had been to church with the padres.

"You mustn't become a Christian," his mother had pleaded.

"Don't trust these foreign padres, they're trying to take you away from us. Oh! What will I do, my son, when you leave us?"

"I'll never leave you, mother," said Rangu. "Even if I become a Christian I shall always belong to you."

"Oh, please, my son, don't say you are going to change your religion. You're not going to leave the faith of your fathers, your uncles, your aunties, your cousins, and, above all, of your dear mother? Rangu, my first-born, what will happen to me when I die?"

"What do you mean, mother?"

"Who will set fire to my funeral pyre, my child? It's the duty of the eldest son, and you know that these fat-bellied Brahmins will never allow a Christian to do this sacred duty."

"Oh! please mother, don't talk to me of death. You frighten me."

"I shan't, my son, if you promise not to change your religion."

Rangu was greatly touched by his mother's words, and he stood there as if rooted to the ground.

"Now, Rangu," she said, "go to your books. You have your exam, next week."

Rangu sat for his examination and passed with honours. It was the eighth standard, and he was awarded the English School Leaving Certificate. This qualified him for a mediocre job. His ambitions were limited and he had no desire to proceed with his studies.

From then, he attended the school as an old boy and a friend of the junior staff, now and again taking the place of an absent master in the lower school, and helping in the general administration of the institution.

The management were proud of the finished product they had made of the crude metal that was once a blacksmith, and when a vacancy occurred in the clerical establishment of the school, they appointed Rangu as assistant clerk. Rangu's wish, however, was to enter the permanent teaching staff.

True, he had achieved something wonderful. Before his appointment it was unthinkable for a blacksmith to become a clerk in a secondary school. The illiterate would now look up to him, but they would respect him more if he became a teacher. They venerated knowledge and would refer to him by a term equivalent to 'professor'.

One day, Rangu suddenly decided to become a Christian and was baptised and admitted a member of the Church. His father was furious and his mother sorely grieved. His enemies scorned him. "You slave of padres," they called him.

Many reasons were adduced for Rangu's change of religion. Some said this and some said that.

"He's ambitious and he wants to get a promotion and so he's pleasing the padres. But he could have got his promotion without changing his religion, or he could have got a job in an office, the pariah fellow," they abused him.

"He's a low-born fellow, such a fellow always shows the baseness of his birth. He's a pariah blacksmith. He likes to be a slave," said a few others.

"He's honest. He had a call from the true God," said his school associates.

However, his enemies were jealous of Rangu and envied his position in the school. They hated him and resented his success. Any reminder of his position in the school pierced them like the thrust of a dagger.

One evening, they assembled together and discussed ways and means of deposing Rangu from his eminence. The man who hated Rangu most spoke first. He suggested that they should send a petition to the Principal of the school alleging that Rangu was a rogue and a hypocrite and that in reality he was a Hindu but pretended to be a Christian to his masters. They could easily find instances in Rangu's life to reinforce their accusation.

"We must plan this out very carefully," said one of the men, "this may not have much effect. Don't forget, friends, Rangu was appointed a clerk before he changed his religion. The change of religion may not be as important as we're trying to make out. Think, brothers, think of the Hindus, few though they be, who are holding good posts in the school. Let's not run foolishly. Let's think and ponder before we act."

"I agree with both of you," remarked another man, "but I may tell you this. Now that Rangu is a Christian, if we send a petition to say that he's not really a Christian, but a hypocrite, a rogue, a pretender and a trickster, that's sure to have effect. Don't forget, brothers, how distasteful hypocrisy, pretence, dishonesty and trickery are to the Christians. I'm certain the petition will work. I can take any bet the pariah blacksmith will be dismissed. Siva! Siva! He will be dismissed!"

"Correctly spoken, brother, correctly spoken," they all shouted with the exception of the second speaker.

It was agreed to send the petition, and they fixed a day when they would meet again and jointly draw up their accusations against Rangu.

As they departed, one of them said, "The petition must be unsigned. It should be anonymous." "Of course, of course," they all shouted together. And their eyes betrayed a vague fear.

The Principal at first ignored the petition. For one thing, it was anonymous and he was suspicious of unsigned documents. For another, the accusation was not sufficiently convincing to make punishment possible. Such accusations could be made against anybody and it was difficult to single out one and prove him guilty. These are matters to be left entirely to the honesty of the individual.

But the petitions came pouring into the office. He was simply pestered and so, one day, in sheer exasperation, he sent for the assistant clerk.

Rangu, however, denied the truth of the allegations and, on the following Sunday, when the pastor at the end of the service suggested that a member of the Church should pray, Rangu responded to the call by offering prayers.

Everything went on smoothly for some time until Rangu's enemies made fresh accusations. They accused Rangu of saying "Siva, Siva," very often. "The name of Siva is always on his lips, not the name of Christ." A new series of petitions poured into the Principal's office.

The Principal, who was feeling relieved that the annoying letters had stopped, began to lose his temper on receiving the new series. He didn't read them properly, but only glanced at the scrawls. The head of the school had very little time.

One of the petitions reached him on a Saturday which he had set apart for Tamil literature. He would rather have read the works of Thiru Valluvar than the illegible scrawls of the anonymous petitioners. He called the Vice-Principal, handed him the letter, and asked him to read it.

The Vice-Principal had been in the country only a month, and the accusation made against Rangu seemed to him monstrous. He thought he should investigate the matter at the earliest opportunity. The next day he called on Rangu.

"Good afternoon, sir," Rangu said.

"Good afternoon, Rangu."

"Wait a moment, sir, I'll bring a chair," said Rangu, and he turned to go into his hut to look for one.

"Never mind about a chair. I'm in a hurry. And I've something very important here," said the Vice-Principal, pulling out a letter from his pocket.

He handed the petition to Rangu and asked: "Is this true?"

Rangu nervously received the letter, and while reading it began to tremble. He became excited and cried: "It's not true, sir! It's not true!"

"Why should they write that if it's not true?" growled the Vice-Principal.

"They're jealous of me Sir. They hate me because I'm doing well and they're also angry with the Principal for giving me the job. Please, sir, I beg you, don't believe them. They only want me to work as a blacksmith," Rangu cried again after a short pause. "They are evil-minded people, sir. Never believe those rascals." And, shaking his clenched fist, he continued, "If only I get a chance I'll teach them a lesson."

Then, throwing his hands in the air, he blurted out, "Siva, Siva, how can I forget Jesus Christ!"

On hearing these words the Vice-Principal's face flushed red, and when Rangu proceeded to explain further, he said, "That'll do. I've heard enough." And he walked angrily out of the smithy.

Rangu ran after the Vice-Principal and, holding him by the arm, implored, "Please don't be angry, sir. How have I offended you? Please come back to the smithy, and I'll explain everything."

"I don't want to hear any more from you," shouted the VicePrincipal and, withdrawing his arm forcibly, he walked away.

Rangu stood there perplexed and then ran back to his house wringing his hands, and shouting, "Siva, Siva, I'm ruined!"

The Vice-Principal went straight back to his superior and excitedly told him what had happened. But he was surprised to find that the Principal did not show any resentment at Rangu's offence. He was puzzled that the Principal should laugh so loudly - as if it were all a big joke.

"You're new to this place," said the Principal. "Excuse my laughter. You'll see the funny side of it later on. You must be tired now: you'd better go and rest."

Rangu, who had spent a restless night, went to the office and worked like mad. He was worried about his future. He vaguely realised that he had committed some offence, but did not know exactly what it was.

The Principal and the Vice-Principal were punctual. Rangu's hands shook and his writing began to scrawl. The Principal noticed this from his desk. He went to the assistant clerk and handed him a letter.

Rangu was surprised. This had never happened before. He trembled as he opened the letter. He read it.

Rangu closed his eyes, opened them, and read again.

It was true! What he had first read was true. He had been promoted to the teaching staff, to fill a vacancy.

He was so happy. He could not control himself.

"Oh, I'm glad," he said. "Thank you, sir, thank you very much!" And, waving the letter aloft, he shouted,

"Siva, Siva. I'll never forget Jesus Christ!"

The Vice-Principal stared at him, and then at his superior.

The Principal turned aside to hide his mirth.

THE MARKET SQUARE

ON their way back, Jaffna bullocks instinctively know that they are returning home. Soon their work will come to an end, at least temporarily, so they run faster, sometimes they even gallop. But the tilk! tilk! tilk! of the carter does not cease however fast they run. He does it by force of habit. He does it as often on the way back as on the outward journey. Moreover, the bullocks, even when they are returning home, do not keep the same pace throughout the entire journey. They simply cannot. It is impossible. Even bullocks can get tired. So they are kicked between their legs, on their behinds. They are beaten on their bellies with a cane which invariably leaves an imprint. Their tails are twisted, and sometimes when the carter is not satisfied with their speed, he crushes their tails between his teeth.

Subbu, the carter, was therefore not being unduly cruel when he shouted at his bullocks. They took the hint and galloped and the uneven road made the cart jerk. It shook Mrs. Ramaswamy. Her reverie was disturbed.

"Don't drive them fast, there's no hurry."

"I am not driving them, I am not even beating them," replied the carter, "they are running of their own accord, they know they are returning home, the beasts. Titk! tilk! tilk!" The bullocks ran. Mrs. Ramaswamy leaned against the side of the cart and returned to her thoughts.

"Tilk! tilk! tilk!" the carter produced the sounds in his mouth but did not repeat them as he thought he heard his mistress crying. The carter held the reins firmly and turned round. Mrs. Ramaswamy was sobbing with her face buried in her arm. "Don't cry, mother, don't cry," the carter said, "your daughter will be happy in the school."

His mistress started to cry louder.

"Don't cry, mother, please don't cry," the carter begged her again, but finding that his requests were of no avail, he pulled up the cart. He then got down from the vehicle and resting his elbows on his seat, he stood facing his mistress.

"Why mother, why are you crying? I really can't understand all this fuss, mother. Why, you are crying as if somebody had died in your family."

"My child! my child!" cried Mrs. Ramaswamy, "Parvati, my child, how am I going to pass my days without you?"

"Siva, Siva, this is a nuisance," cried the carter, holding the reins in one hand, and beating his head with the other. "Siva! Siva!"

Soon the carter realised that his intervention only made matters worse, so he mounted his seat and drove on.

"Tilk! tilk! tilk!" He twisted the tails of the animals in his hands, kicked their behinds and tried to reproduce his sounds louder than before. He wanted to drown Mrs. Ramaswamy's sobs and moans. And he did succeed to some extent. They were now nearing the market place and the carter again stopped the vehicle on the side of the road. "You must stop this, mother," he begged, "we are nearing the market place, it is a crowded area, and if you go on crying, all those ruffians will crowd round the cart."

"Subbu, don't stop the cart where there are too many people, you know I dislike crowds."

"You may dislike crowds, but you are going to have them all right," replied the carter, somewhat rudely.

"Why, why do you say that?"

"Because you are crying, you are making a scene and those ruffians in the market place only wait for a chance to assemble together to make a fuss and crack dirty jokes."

"Don't talk rubbish, Subbu," said Mrs. Ramaswamy, wiping her eyes with the edge of her sari. The carter smiled triumphantly and drove on.

"Tilk! tilk! tilk!"

"I am not talking rubbish, mother," he said, starting to speak again, "I may be your servant, but I have more experience than you. Don't forget, mother, I served your mother and I knew you as an infant in arms."

"You are talking like a father, Subbu."

"Of course, I am like a father to you, mother, though I call you mother. I have carried you in my arms in the days when I was your mother's servant and called her mother. Then I used to call you by your name. Now I am your servant and wouldn't dare to address you by your name."

"You are becoming too difficult to understand. I have never heard you talk like this, Subbu. Please don't talk in that manner. I can't worry my head to understand you. I am too unhappy to think hard. My daughter is separated from me and here you are talking to me in riddles!"

Hardly had the carter had time to think over his mistress's reply when Mrs. Ramaswamy burst into tears.

"My only child, my dear pet, my own Parvati, how am I going to pass my days without you? I shan't see you for three months, and it's going to be like three years to me," she moaned.

"What's this? What's all this? We are near the market place and you are making a fuss. Siva! Siva!" cried the carter.

They were now near the Grand Bazaar, and the carter stopped the cart on the side of the road at some distance from the market.

"There, mother, see the crowds there, and that is the marketplace. "The market is in the square there. We'll have to pass that place and unless you stop crying I won't proceed farther."

Mrs. Ramaswamy remembered what the carter had told her about the ruffians, and so with a deliberate effort she stopped crying.

"Tilk! tilk! tilk!" Subbu drove on, proud of the way he had averted a public exhibition of his mistress's emotions.

"I don't mind your crying, mother," said Subbu after a pause, attempting to explain, "but you know how these town rowdies behave; you see they are worse than our village loafers. Besides, in the village nobody would dare to make a rude remark to you, because you are the wife of the headman, but here it is different, mother. I hope you understand, I beg your pardon for my interference, and if you can't pardon me, you can deduct twenty-five cents from my salary when I get my pay." He emphasised the word 'when' sarcastically.

"It's all right, Subbu, I understand you, you are an experienced man, you are much older than me, and you should guide me."

"I don't mind your crying, mother," the carter repeated, "but you must control yourself, at least, here in Grand Bazaar. When these rowdies hear you crying, they will crowd round the cart and one man will say this, and another man will say that, but they will all be agreed on one thing. May their bodies rot, the wretches!"

"What is it? Why are you angry?"

"Do you know, mother, do you know what these rowdies will say? They will suggest that I tried to do something to you, and that is why you are crying. And even if I swear by the life of my own mother I never attempted to do anything to you, they will with one voice shout me down and call the police. And with the police I'll be more truthful and swear, not by the life of my mother who is dead, but by Siva. Even so the police won't believe me, they will beat me with their sticks, handcuff me and drag me to the police station."

"Don't talk nonsense, you are like a father to me. You are an old man, you'd never do a thing like that."

"Sure, I'll never do that to you, mother. By Siva, I'll never. But all the same, I am not too old, mother," replied the carter, peeved at the suggestion that he was incapable, "if you ask big-breasted grass-seller, she will tell you of my strength, she will."

"My God, Subbu, I never dreamt that you were such a bad man. Subbu, do you really ...?"

"No, mother, I was only fooling you," replied the carter with a tremor in his voice.

They now reached the square where the market was held, and the carter slowed down. A woman with a child in her arms ran after the cart and cried: "Please give some alms. Look, mother, an infant!"

The carter turned back and scolded her.

"Please, mother, please give a cent. The child is starving I shall pray that one day you become a Maharanee."

"Run away, or I'll measure your height with my stick," shouted the carter.

Marakayer, a stealer and mender of umbrellas, stood right in front of the cart and exhibited his umbrellas.

"It's going to rain hard. The astrologer says that there will be a storm, with thunder and lightning. Even Lord Indra, God of the Rain, Thunder and Lightning, will not be able to stop it. Woe unto those who haven't umbrellas. Buy them immediately and from me, Marakayer, Prince of Umbrellas."

"Prince of Umbrellas! Oh, you liar! You mean stealer of umbrellas," shouted a man who stood nearby as he cleared his throat and spat contemptuously at Marakayer.

"Run away, you dirty swine! You son of a ..." bawled Marakayer, as he raised one of his umbrellas to strike the man, who ran to a safe distance and spat again.

The bullocks were terrified at the sight of the black umbrellas and refused to move. "Tilk! tilk! tilk!" Still they declined to budge. The carter kicked their behinds, twisted their tails, then bit them, and, in exasperation, even spat on them, yet he couldn't persuade them to step forward. At each beating, they raised their heads and contracted their backs and the cart began to move backwards.

"Subbu, stop on a side where there aren't too many people. I would like to see what is happening here. Perhaps we could buy something if it is cheap."

"Move on, you wretched fellow," shouted the carter. "Don't you know, you rascal, that bullocks are scared of black cloth, and if you stand there-with those black umbrellas, I can't drive."

"Mind your words," said Marakayer, "I have made younger and more robust men than you measure their lengths on the ground."

"Tilk! tilk! tilk! You son of a prostitute, I'll measure your height with my stick!"

"Mind your words, I warn you again," said Marakayer, and he threatened to strike the carter with an umbrella.

Mrs. Ramaswamy, who had been trembling all the while, now screamed. The onlookers laughed.

"If you don't put that umbrella down, I'll circumcise you again," cried the carter.

The altercation would have continued, but the chauffeur of the car that was held up because of the bullock cart, grew impatient and blew his horn loudly. Marakayer shamefacedly gave way.

"Tilk! tilk! tilk!" The bullocks drew to a side. The carter got down and looked right ahead at the centre of the market.

"There he is, there's the rogue," he shouted.

"Who?" asked his mistress.

"The renter of the market, the rogue who collects the money from the vendors. I'll run up and ask him if we can park the cart here."

He stepped into the square. The bullocks started to move.

"Hey, Subbu, the bullocks are moving! Come here and save me. My God, they are going to drag me into a bottomless pit. Come, Subbu, come quickly!"

The carter held his dhoti up and ran back.

"Ah, there he is, there's the rogue."

"Who, Subbu?"

"The rogue of a renter, Hay Raman."

The renter was on his usual round collecting rents. He thanked his prompt payers and patted them on their backs. The defaulters he abused mercilessly and in some cases confiscated a part or whole of their goods. He was also the owner of a hay shop close to the market. It was, at the same time, a rendezvous for the ruffians of the neighbourhood, who sat on stacks of hay, smoked cigars, compared notes on the scandals of the town and versified them. Their latest victim was a young nautch girl whom they nicknamed 'Cycle' because her lovers were mostly undergraduates who, when they were not with her, rode on bicycles. Her mother was called 'Bus' because her customers were bus drivers.

"You mustn't call him Hay Raman," said Mrs. Ramaswamy to the carter.

"Why not, mother?"

"Because, if that is his nickname he may get annoyed and won't help us."

"It is not his nickname it's his name. You see, mother, he owns a hay-shop, but no hay ever gets sold there."

"What happens, Subbu?"

"Something else happens, but I won't tell you, mother. It would frighten you."

"You have already frightened me, Subbu, Now tell me what happens? Oh, this is a terrible place, and I am leaving my child, and that, too, a girl, in this horrible town. Oh, my poor child, my Parvati."

"Now, now, don't cry, mother."

"Oh, my child, my child," cried Mrs. Ramaswamy loudly.

"Siva! Siva! What am I going to do? The rowdies are coming!" cried the carter.

Mrs. Ramaswamy immediately stopped crying and wiped her tears. The carter's eyes gleamed triumphantly.

"Hoi, Hay!" shouted the carter.

"What is it? What do you want?"

"Come here, Hay, I want to speak to you."

"Don't say anything nasty," said Mrs. Ramaswamy softly to the carter.

The renter went near the cart.

"May we park the cart in some part of the square?"

"You'll have to pay a rupee," replied Raman.

"Come here, Hay, I want to tell you something," the carter whispered something into the renter's ear. Raman peeped into the cart and looked at Mrs. Ramaswamy and surveyed her sari.

"Wife of a headman!" whispered the carter again.

"All right, take the beasts along to the square. I shan't charge you anything this time." He faced Mrs. Ramaswamy. "My market will be honoured by your presence, mother."

Mrs. Ramaswamy got down from the cart and thanked him. The renter joined his hands and bowed. The carter led the bullocks to the square.

"Let us go to the market, Subbu," said Mrs. Ramaswamy as soon as the carter was back.

A middle-aged man came running to Mrs. Ramaswamy, stood in front of her, joined his hands and said, "Come to my stall, mother, I have lots of things, mother. Bangles, combs and toys. Very nice articles, all from Yapan. You should buy some for the children."

"Yes, mother, let us go and look at his things," Subbu said, and then softly, "it is not necessary to buy anything."

When they reached the stall, the man offered the visitor an empty wooden box, and suggested that she might sit on it. Subbu sat on the ground. The keeper of the stall pestered Mrs. Ramaswamy to buy something, and she bought a cheap comb to avoid further trouble.

"Here you are, Subbu, you can give this to your grass-seller."

The carter felt it in his hand and remarked, "This won't do for that elephant. This will break the moment it touches her porcupine quills."

His mistress laughed and thought of her own mass of sleek blue-black hair. The stall-holder repeated the carter's remark and looked at him angrily.

"It won't break," he said, "it is very strong, it is Yapan-make. You can comb the thorny bushes of the jungle with it."

Mrs. Ramaswamy smiled and raised her eyebrows. "Keep it, Subbu," she said, "if you don't want it, we can give it to someone else."

A terrific noise now burst upon them. A bus passed by with loud hooting of horns.

"Hoi, Hey!" shouted an old man, "bus going to Karainagar. Villagers returning home. These fellows at one time used to walk to town and back. Now they sit proudly in buses. What has come to the world? May their legs rot! The wretches!"

The occupants of the bus looked out of the window and grinned.

"Wretches, they don't even have the time to answer," said the old man.

"It's because of the speed, brother," replied his companion.

"It's something for the white man to have made the motor car, but how did he manage to put speed into it?" remarked an observant man who stood right in the centre of the market scanning the entire square.

"How did he manage to put speed into it? How did he manage to put speed into it?" a chorus of voices rose into the air.

"How did I manage to put speed into my bullocks?" shouted the carter.

The crowd turned towards him and laughed.

Grey and black clouds drifted slowly across the sky and covered the sun. As the sun disappeared, Marakayer made his appearance.

"Whensoever there is misery and ignorance, I come," he quoted the Gita.

"Who comes?" interrogated the crowd.

"Subramanya," replied Marakayer.

The umbrella-seller knew the tricks of his trade. He knew that to the crowd in the square, who were worshippers of the Saivite pantheon, Krishna meant little. Krishna to the Saivites was a playful boy, who had a beloved called Radha, to whom he had not been very faithful. Marakayer had learned the words from a Brahmin priest to whom he had sold three umbrellas on credit.

"Whensoever there is misery and ignorance, Subramanya comes," Marakayer repeated, modifying the Gita, "but whensoever there is going to be storm, thunder and lightning, Marakayer comes."

"Don't tell lies, you umbrella-stealer," someone said, "there won't be rain. Look, the clouds are drifting away."

"Who said that?" interrogated Marakayer, "I have just consulted the astrologer. He said that we were going to have a heavy storm."

"Subbu! Subbu!" shouted Mrs. Ramaswamy.

"Don't be afraid, he is a liar," said the stall-keeper.

"You rascal," shouted Hay Raman, who now made a sudden appearance, "you haven't paid your rent and have the cheek to insult my honoured visitor. Hold him, all of you!"

Two stalwart men seized Marakayer and held him on the spot while the renter snatched his umbrellas.

"Run away, you umbrella stealer. Go and steal some more umbrellas and come back," said Hay Raman, as he hit Marakayer with an umbrella.

The umbrella broke in two. Marakayer took to his heels.

Subbu now appeared on the scene after wandering through the market.

"Look, mother, look what I have bought."

"What, Subbu?"

"I have bought new jewellery for our bullocks. I got them very cheap, they are gilded. Bells, necklaces and these for the horns."

"You are a good man, Subbu. I'll ask my man to pay you when we reach home."

"That will never happen, mother. Anyway I shan't ask him. For if I do, he will only scold me. He would say that I was wasting his daughter's dowry."

The carter noticed that his mistress was thinking of her daughter at the mention of the word 'dowry'.

"Let us go," he said, "you never know when it will rain. True the clouds are parting, but you can never be certain of anything, mother."

"Tilk! tilk! tilk!" The bullocks trotted, cantered and then galloped. The bells round their necks tinkled.' The jewels on their horns gave them a raised effect like the double plaits on a woman's head. They were beaten and kicked and their tails twisted, yet they didn't mind as they seemed to be pre-occupied with their new ornaments. Their bellies shook rhythmically like the rounded breasts of a mature temple dancer. They ran self-consciously, proudly and hopefully to their destination, unheedful of the carter.

"Tilk! tilk! tilk!"

THE FLOOD

MY father grumbled and complained; although he did not go to court on Saturdays, it was on this day that he received the proctors and litigants. There was a storm with thunder and lightning and neither the proctors nor the clients called. It meant a decline in his practice the coming week.

Saturday was a day full of interest for me too, and I always looked forward to it. But the rain interfered with my activities. My mother would not let me go out. She wrapped me in a large blanket and put woollen socks on my feet and a monkey-cap on my head. I prayed for the rain to cease, so that I might be able to go out with my friend and catch butterflies.

A short distance from our house and in the same street lived Sethu Lakshmi Ammal, who owned a grocery store. She was a widow with three children and resided in a small hut. She slaved from dawn till late at night-a big, clumsy old woman, with a chapped face and masses of unkempt hair, always grumbling and groaning. Sometimes, she would become hysterical and scream at her customers and neighbours.

Her speciality was a kind of pancake called *thosai*. Flour, mashed lentils and coconut-milk were mixed together to form a liquid paste. Two or three spoonfuls of this were transferred to a griddle and baked. Sethu was famous for these pancakes, and men, women and children went joyfully to her shop. Sometimes, she hardly had room to accommodate all of them. Her small hut was partitioned in two; the part closer to the road served both as grocery and bakery, and, in the other, she slept and kept her things. Her customers were poor and bought their groceries in small quantities.

Chasing butterflies, beads of perspiration streamed down our backs. So we went to the grocery shop, to rest for a while and eat pancakes. Sometimes, when we had two or three cents between us, we gave them to Sethu; but more often, we pinched her *thosais*, while she was busy attending to other customers. Whenever she caught us in the act, she threatened to beat us and vowed never to let us enter her shop again.

My friend and I teased Sethu quite a lot. At night, the old woman lit her primitive lamp. She had made it herself, by filling a small bottle with kerosene, fitting it with a metal-stopper and inserting a piece of rag through the stopper, to serve as the wick. While I stood and watched, my friend would steal in and blow out the lamp. Then we would both run, as the old woman cursed and swore at us.

But Sethu was at heart a kind and accommodating sort. Those who went to her were very poor and she often supplied them groceries on credit.

"I'm silly to do it!" she would grumble. "I'm a fool. But when a child comes for a loaf of bread and I have the bread and know her family is starving, how can I refuse? Yet, I have my own children to think of! I am being ruined!"

I now longed to go and see Sethu, but the rain showed no signs of stopping. My mother brought me a cup of tea, with more milk in it than tea, and I realised, to my chagrin, that it was tea-time and I had lost all chance of catching butterflies and eating pancakes. There was no change in the weather at any time during the day. The outlook was dull and dreary and, soon, it was nightfall. The water had reached the level of our rear veranda.

I went to bed in fear, folding my legs together, with the knees almost touching my chin. When I woke up in the morning, it was still raining. The whole place was flooded and water had risen higher and higher during the night.

I looked out of the window and saw a dead dog floating and, a little farther, a cat, some fowl and chickens. During the night, many houses had crumbled and quite a few lives had been lost. Residents on our road came to our house. Our immediate neighbours occupied one section of the building; the barber, the washerman, the blacksmith and other workmen also came to us for shelter.

But everybody forgot Sethu Lakshmi Ammal, Not one of the many persons who had enjoyed eating Sethu's pancakes cared to remember her on this day. I ran to my mother and asked her to send someone to bring Sethu.

"How can I ask anybody to go out in this storm, my son?" she said. "It is raining hard. What can I do!? What about her grown-up children? Surely, they can help her!"

"But, mother, they are not in Jaffna. They are employed as servants somewhere a long way off."

"Please be quiet," she said. "It is impossible to send anyone now." And she bent down and pulled my socks up.

Meanwhile, the weather did not improve, and, on the third day, a storm of unusual fury burst on the town and raged for many hours. The thunder was deafening-the crash of the waves on the beach, the howling of the wind through the palms and coconut trees, and the beating of rain. Every time the rain slackened for a few minutes, we hoped that the storm had passed, but another clap of thunder announced its return. The inhabitants became nervous and almost distraught. "Oh, Lord Indra, God of the Rains, Thunder and Lightning, please stop the rain, we beg you," they all cried.

I could not sleep for a long time that night and clung closely to my mother. Now and again, she extricated herself from my clasp and went in search of basins and other utensils for collecting the water that was seeping in through the tiles. "Sleep, sleep, my child," she said. Don't be frightened; everything will be right tomorrow. It is not raining very hard now."

When I woke up next day, everybody was rejoicing. For though the sky was still grey, and the clouds hung low, the rain had stopped. But it was not until the sixth day that anybody ventured out. The inspectors of roads and drains, assisted by the local police, worked hard, clearing, repairing and building. Life in the town slowly returned to its normal routine and, at nine in the morning, I went to the Tamarind School, taking in my bag my mother's solutions of the homework set for me! I was accompanied by my friend.

But on our way this time, we missed the familiar figure of Sethu. On the spot where her grocery shop had stood, we saw a group of men talking to one another, almost in whispers. We approached them and enquired after Sethu. Some of them waved us aside and turned their heads away sorrowfully, while others scolded us for being inquisitive, and suggested we run to school, if we didn't want to be late.

From that day onwards, whenever we passed that way, we often turned to look for the grocery shop, but we never saw Sethu Lakshmi Ammal again, nor did we have any more opportunities of teasing her or benefiting from her sense of generosity.

THE FAN

THE headmaster was a broad-shouldered man with a fan constantly in his right hand. He was suffering from catarrh and the soft blowing of the air, caused by the gentle movement of the fan, temporarily eased his ailment. At one moment he would seem perfectly normal, then, a sudden fit of sneezing would seize him. It shook his body, exhausted him, and its noise reverberated in the adjoining classrooms. He then worked his fan and the resulting breeze soothed him and arrested the recurrence of his sneeze.

He spent the day sneezing, teaching and punishing his pupils, and fanning himself. His work was in the upper forms, but he went round the whole school to supervise the work of his assistants, hear complaints and punish the delinquents. On first offenders he used the thin long handle of his fan; on habituals and incorrigibles he used the cane. "This time the fan, next time the cane," he always repeated as he held his fan upside down and dug into the ribs of his victims with the pointed end, or beat them on their flanks.

The boys in his classes were always alert and prepared their lessons diligently. He was an expert in mathematics and knew Nesfield's English Grammar by heart. His writing was as clear as his brain and his characters were gracefully formed. It was an aesthetic delight to watch him solve problems on the blackboard. He was clever, humorous and cruel. He canvassed the attention of his students with his fan, the cane and his wit. His assistants dreaded and respected him.

But nobody feared the headmaster more than Mylan, a farmer's son. Mylan helped his father before going to school. He was an assiduous worker. At five o'clock every morning his mother pulled him out of bed. He rinsed his mouth, ate a handful of leftovers from the previous night's meal, and then partnered his father in the open.

Mylan was indispensable to his father. Although he was helpless at drawing water from a deep well, he was quite smart at other jobs. He made a thorough survey of the plantation, prevented the water from overflowing and breaking the sandbanks, removed the weeds and the rubbish, built fresh sandbanks, collected the fallen coconuts together into a heap, plucked the rotten leaves from the banana trees. All this and more besides.

The farmer's boy walked two miles every day to school. To avoid being late he was sometimes constrained to run parts of this distance. At such times he regretted that he was not as fortunate as his classmates, Kirupa and Ranjan.

Kirupa, the son of a high court judge from the neighbouring town, came to school in his father's car. At the scheduled time a maroon limousine, with Kirupa as its sole passenger, entered smoothly and majestically the portals of the school. He wore short trousers and shirt, gold bangles and Roman sandals. His long brown hair was parted on a side and cascaded in curls down his profile. Mylan evinced great admiration for Kirupa and tried to befriend him. Ranjan was a chubby-faced lad with close-cropped hair. A nearly naked coolie, his dark sweating body gleaming in the morning sun, transported him to school in a rickshaw. He was a proud little upstart and felt superior as he sat cross-legged in the man-propelled vehicle. Unlike Kirupa who often played with Mylan, Ranjan, the diminutive snob, kept himself aloof. He had even advised the judge's son not to associate with the shabby peasant boy.

Mylan's morning work took more time on some days than on others, and he arrived at the school late by a few minutes. He had already been punished twice by his class master. His work in the field had detained him on both these occasions, but his teacher did not consider that as a reasonable excuse. Little Mylan had run as fast as his thin legs could carry him and had arrived at the school panting and late by ten minutes. Only ten minutes late, and yet he had been ordered on the first occasion to stay outside the class; on the second to stand on the bench for the rest of the lesson. The headmaster, while on his morning tour of inspection, had pointed his fan at him and had severely warned him.

"Mylan! Mylan! Mylan!" called his mother one morning earlier than usual. That day's assignment was an extraordinary piece of luck. The landed proprietor of the village had engaged the services of the farmer and his son for a week. His estate had been neglected for some time and needed immediate repair.

The boy's parents considered this unexpected work as a godsend, especially his mother who had been eagerly looking forward to her husband getting additional employment. She longed to buy a new 'dhoti' for Mylan, and she intended to reserve the money the landed proprietor would pay the toilers entirely for her son's needs. She realised that the week's wages would be small, for farmers are seldom equitably remunerated. But the proprietor was a rich man and, in her simple mind, she naively imagined that such a man would be generous. And she soared skyward on a rocket of surprise and delight.

The field was large and the work was arduous. But Mylan was more energetic that day, for in the course of his labours he recollected his mother's promise. The landed proprietor supervised the work from his bungalow. His fat wife stood by like a wine barrel without legs. They were keen that the clearing should be completed quickly so that in the evenings, after the sun had set, they could saunter leisurely in the field and breathe the cool fresh air in the open.

Mylan's work was not confined to one place, sometimes he was out of sight from his father who began to wonder if his son had slipped away.

"Oh Myla! Oi Mylan! Ohe Myloo! Where have you gone? Where have you drifted, you lazy fellow? Where have you died?" came the hoarse voice of the farmer penetrating the coconut palms, past the mango groves and reaching the farthest end of the estate where Mylan was. He responded to the call and was soon by his father's side.

It was now time for him to go home and prepare for school. On his way back he wondered if it were late and was terrified at the thought. While working in the field the world of classes and masters seemed very far off, but now as he scurried homewards, the figure of the headmaster advancing with his fan took shape in his mind and frightened him. In the distance he saw his mother waiting for him outside their house. She ran to meet her son halfway, took him affectionately in her arms and kissed him on both cheeks.

On reaching the school Mylan was perturbed at the absence of the maroon car. It had come and gone a long while ago, for when he went to his class the first lesson was already over. He was afraid to enter and while he stood there perplexed, he heard the footsteps of the headmaster approaching and his whole body trembled. Mylan tried to give an explanation for his tardiness, but the headmaster would not listen to him. He was impatient and irritable as he was suffering from a severe attack of catarrh that day.

"No excuses," he said, "you are always late. This time fan, next time the cane." He thrust the sharp end of the fan into Mylan. The boy sobbed and groaned with pain.

The next day Mylan refused to attend school, and when his mother admonished him, he showed her the wound on his chest and cried "Oh my mother! Oh my mother! Look what the headmaster did to me!"

When his father came home in the afternoon and saw that his son had played truant, he reprimanded him, but when he attempted to drag him away, Mylan ran to his mother and clinging closely to her cried, "Oh my mother! Oh my mother! The fan ... The fan ... next time the cane."

PROFESSIONAL MOURNERS

MY grandmother died late at night on a Saturday while my sister, brother and I were fast asleep. We were wakened in the morning by the cries from grandmother's house and the sound of drums. We dressed hurriedly and ran to her place. A large gathering was there and the space between the boundary fence and the outer verandah was lined with people. We pushed our way through the crowd to the centre of the hut in search of our mother. We were feeling afraid because it was the first funeral we had attended.

We had hardly entered grandmother's house when we heard the shouts of the 'Master of Ceremonies', who was in charge of all arrangements on such occasions. He was our uncle, a teacher in a small school, and a trifle mad. He always spoke rapidly and loudly. And when he was angry he would shout at the top of his voice until the whole village heard him. This morning he was furious because the professional mourners had not yet arrived. "I'll go and fetch them myself," he said, and stamped out of the house. I left my brother and sister, and ran after him, as I was anxious to see the mourners about whom I had heard many stories.

We walked through sandy lanes and narrow winding footpaths. There were no dwelling houses about and no noise, though I thought I heard the hissing of snakes under the bushes and the howling of jackals in the distance. "The snakes won't bite you; don't be afraid, "my uncle reassured me.

Presently we arrived at a row of huts near the seashore. By the beach stood fishermen, some mending their nets, assisted by their wives, others on the point of putting their catamarans to sea.

"Stop, stop, you stupid rascals," cried my uncle as he ran up to them. "Don't you know that my aunt's funeral is to take place today? You low-minded fellows! You should be there instead of on the seashore."

"We didn't know about it," they said, as they left their fishing nets and catamarans. "We shall be there soon." They clasped their hands and bent down.

Admonishing them again, my uncle walked on in search of the mourners. "That is where these wretched women live," he said, pointing to a few huts even smaller than the ones we had left behind.

He stopped outside and called to the inmates. Two women, dressed in coarse saris which did not come over their shoulders or heads, came out. They wore bangles from their wrists to their elbows, and anklets that jingled as they came forward. He shouted at them angrily: "I sent word to you that my aunt's funeral will take place today. Why haven't you come all this time?"

"We were getting ready to come, master: please pardon us for being late," said one of them.

"Where are the other mourners?" growled the Master of Ceremonies.

"There are only two of them here at the moment, sir, two sisters. We don't know where the rest are, but even these two cannot come as their mother died this morning, and they will have to attend the funeral."

"Nonsense! Where do these wretches live?" he demanded.

"Not far from here, sir."

"Lead me there!"

The two women led the way and we followed them. They stopped outside a hut and yelled for the two sisters who came out, tying the upper part of their saris which had slipped down over their pointed breasts.

They stopped suddenly, stared for a moment, and then prostrated themselves before the Master, saying, "Please excuse us today, sir. Our mother died this morning and we are too much overcome with grief to come and cry at the funeral of outsiders."

"Impudence!" cried the Master. "Two mourners are not enough for my aunt's funeral. Remember who she is."

"Please excuse them," said the mourner who acted as the spokesman. "It is not fair, as they will have to shed tears of genuine sorrow on the loss of their mother instead of pretending at your place."

I noticed that the lips of my kinsman were trembling and his eyes were dilated. The woman who had spoken looked down. I shook my head in sympathy. The Master's anger was now diverted to me, rushing like water through fresh sandbanks.

"Don't be a silly fool," he scolded. "What do you know of these things? Your father's lawyer friends are expected. His Honour the Supreme Court Judge and the Police Magistrate are coming, and what will they think about us if we don't have enough mourners?"

The sisters, still on bended knees, begged to be excused. "We didn't mean to be rude, sir," said one of them, "but please let us go this time. On the next occasion when there is another funeral at your place we will come and howl until our throats give way!"

"Insolence!" shouted my uncle. "So you are wishing for another death in my house. Probably you desire mine, you miserable creatures! I'll have you flogged by the magistrate for such impudence." And getting hold of their saris he dragged them along the ground for some distance.

"Please remove your hand; we are coming," they wailed.

The Master of Ceremonies released them and strode forward leaving the four mourners and myself to bring up the rear.

On reaching grandmother's house the women threw their hands in the air, unfastened their hair, and began to cry. They joined other women relatives and friends, who sat crying in groups of two's and three's with their heads resting on each other's necks. The professional mourners sat down a short distance away from the others and, throwing their hands in the air, now beating their heads, now their breasts, began to wail and moan. They spoke as they cried, using various expressions in praise of grandmother. In the course of their professional duty they heard some of the genuine weepers whispering that grandmother might have been taken away from us long ago, but the great god Siva had spared her till cousin Thampoo, her favourite grandson, returned from Malaya. This gave them a new slogan. They rose from the carpet, ruffled their hair, crossed their arms, beat their shoulders and cried:

"Your grandson has come, wake up, my beloved!
Yourgrand son has come, wake up, my darling!"

Meanwhile, the Master of Ceremonies had boasted of his great deed to his friends who, contrary to his expectations, were horrified at his cruelty. They protested against the inhuman act of the Master, who was forced to apologise to the two mourners. Many of the guests, too, offered their condolences to the sisters, and my father, after promising to compensate them adequately, told them to go home.

Now that the Master of Ceremonies had been reprimanded, the women preferred to wait till the entire ceremony was over, declaring that they might as well stay a little longer and give the full benefit of their services.

The Master, on the other hand, since an action of his had been severely criticised, tried to make up for it by undertaking extra work and engaged himself more busily in his duties than before. He scolded the drummers for slacking, ridiculed them because they could not even drown the voices of the professional mourners, and exhorted them to beat faster and louder. Then he carried bags full of rice, packets of incense and other ceremonial necessities to the bedside of the corpse. By this time he was tired and panting. The effort, following on the walk to fetch the mourners, had exhausted him. Suddenly he fainted and fell flat on the ground. Some of the visitors shrieked, while others ran to his help, carried him to a corner, washed his face with water, and fanned him. In a few moments he recovered, apologised, and said he would get up soon. His friends assured him that there were others to help in the arrangements and asked him to rest for some time.

The two sisters among the mourners, whose voices had till now lacked their usual intensity, rose and rent the air with their shrill cries, quite unconcerned about the fate of the Master of Ceremonies. The four mourners now worked in unison, their bodies swaying like reeds in the wind, and lamented in chorus:

"The poor will miss you, oh, you charitable one!
Who is going to feed us on festival days?
Your grandson has come, wake up, my beloved!
Your grandson has come, wake up, my darling!"

After a while their lamentations waned, but there was a fresh outburst when the priest arrived. This was followed by a lull to enable him to perform the religious ceremony.

During the ceremony the priest became curious about the repeated mention of 'grandson' and, being told the story, he called Thampoo to grandmother's bedside to burn some incense and offer prayers. Thampoo, who had maintained an abnormal composure throughout the day, burst into tears just after he had said the prayers.

"You had been waiting for me for many years," he cried. "What fate was it that kept me away? And when I came at last, you lay unconscious on the bed and I was not even able to speak to you."

The mourners took up the theme and wailed:

"Why do you remain silent, mother of a great lawyer?
Answer for the sake of your loved ones!
Open those eyes that are shaped like a fish!
Like those of Minakshi, famed goddess of Madura!
Your grandson has come, wake up, my beloved!
Your grandson has come, wake up, my darling!"

COUSIN THAMPOO

THAMPOO was my father's brother's son. His parents died while he was still a boy, leaving him to be brought up by my father. When he grew up he proceeded to Malaya and secured employment as an engineer. The first time I saw Thampoo was when he came home for his first long holidays. He arrived with easy chairs, China silk and plenty of cash.

Cousin Thampoo regarded my parents as if they were his own and I addressed him as *Annan* (elder brother). Within a few days of his return there were proposals of marriage for him. They were all addressed to my father, as he had taken upon himself the duty of arranging a marriage for his nephew.

From the moment of his arrival, my mother and I made efforts to convert Thampoo to the Christian faith. She wished he should marry a Christian girl and so I took him to St. Peter's Church on Sundays to show him the girls. We sat in the back row and during prayers I pointed out the various girls and whispered to him who they were and what they did at Tamarind. I then closed my eyes, mumbled a few words of prayer and then showed him another girl. But cousin Thampoo never shut his eyes during prayers, nor did he ever ask forgiveness from Jesus for the sins we were committing. Extraordinary, I thought. There we were sitting next to each other, addressing one another as *Annan* and *Thamby* (little brother) and yet we owed allegiance to different gods.

One of the curious things about Ceylon is the ease with which some people move from one religion to another. My mother is a Methodist, her father having been a pastor of a church. My father hails from an orthodox Hindu family, but was baptised before he married my mother. Nowadays inter-religious marriages are a common occurrence and such unions are termed civil marriages.

But the relative of ours who caused the greatest amusement was a cousin of my father. We called him 'Father's Cousin.' He, too, like my father was born to orthodox Hindu parents, but had been baptised before he was appointed headmaster of a Methodist school. When he quarrelled with the management, he renounced Christianity, reverted to Hinduism and accepted a post under the Hindu Board of Education. And when he differed with the Hindu Board he returned to the Methodist. He changed his faith so frequently that it was difficult to know to which religion he belonged and of which school he was the head.

The only grandparent I knew was my father's mother. She was a devout Saivite and often wore the holy ashes.

She admonished my father for changing his religion. "Your father during his lifetime sang hymns in praise of Siva," she said. "You sing 'Onward Christian Soldiers!' Shame on you."

My father never retaliated, but mother and I joined issue with grandmother on the comparative excellences of the two religions. Father's tolerance made us suspicious and we often whispered to each other that he was not a real believer. He was a convert, we were originals.

One day, while Cousin Thampoo and I were taking a walk near the seashore, I said to him, "*Annan*, when are you going to be baptised?"

"Why do you want to know that?"

"Because I would like you to marry a Christian girl."

"Why do you wish that?"

"Because Christian girls are more advanced."

Thampoo laughed. "I can hear your mother talking."

"No," I protested, "but I have noticed in the Tamarind School that Christian girls are more modern than Hindus. Christian girls wear their saris more elegantly, they wear their hair in different styles, they play the piano and they make delicious cakes. If you marry a Hindu girl you will be eating *vadais* all the time."

Cousin Thampoo roared with laughter and began to pat my head. I was annoyed.

"All right," he conceded, "I'll marry a Christian girl, but there is no reason why I should change my religion. I can contract a civil marriage."

"Father has told you all this nonsense," I replied.

He gave me a mischievous smile. My mother and I, however, were determined to go ahead with the work of the Lord. We worked steadily on Thampoo, placing our trust in Jesus. And one day Cousin Thampoo finally agreed to become a convert. A day was fixed for his baptism and my father started to sort out the various proposals of marriage that had come for Thampoo from Christian families.

The baptism day soon arrived. We were getting ready to go to church, when who should come, but grandmother, all the way from her village. She was wearing holy ashes and she looked furious. We lined up on the verandah to listen to her.

"What does all this mean? Making Thampoo a Christian?" she shouted.

"I had nothing to do with it," my father said defensively. My mother and I looked away from grandmother. She demanded, "Who's going to light my funeral pyre?"

"What?"

"Who's going to cremate me when I die?"

My rather turned sadly away from grandmother and my mother and I remained silent. Cousin Thampoo just stood there and looked guilty.

"My own son can't perform my funeral rites," grandmother said, pointing to my father.

"Why?" Thampoo asked.

"Because he's a Christian. Those Brahmin priests won't allow him to perform the funeral rites, nor let him cremate me."

"What is going to happen then?" Cousin Thampoo asked solicitously.

"I have always depended on you to cremate me," grandmother said, "and now even you let me down by becoming a Christian. If my own son can't cremate me, at least my grandson should. If you fail me, to whom shall I go? Outsiders? Shame on the family."

"We'll let father become a Hindu for the occasion," I suggested.

"Shut up! Don't talk rubbish!" grandmother admonished me.

"I have not been baptised yet," Cousin Thampoo admitted weakly.

My mother and I looked at each other. We had no effective answer for grandmother. My father instructed me to go to the pastor and inform him that Cousin Thampoo would not be baptised that day. And so, after all, Thampoo remained a Hindu and married a Saivite girl. We attended the wedding and took part in the ceremonies. 'Father's cousin' became a Hindu for the occasion.

The following Sunday mother and I went for service to St. Peter's Church and we persuaded father to join us. But Cousin Thampoo and his bride stayed at home. We did not ask them to come with us. There was no point in it, now anyhow.

THE BIG GIRL

MRS. Ramaswamy woke up first, smoothed her hair with her hand, arranged her sari and went to wake her husband.

"Please get up," she said. He turned over on his side.

"What's wrong with you today? You always get up when I wake you. Don't forget we haven't much time. I must take Parvati to school."

Her husband turned over again and lay on his back. Mrs. Ramaswamy went to the kitchen. Her husband got out of the bed, went to the compound, and washed himself. He then shouted for his wife. Mrs. Ramaswamy brought him his coffee and he sat down to read the newspaper.

"Oh, Ramaswamy," somebody looked over the fence and greeted the headman, "I hear you're sending your daughter to an English school." Ramaswamy put his paper down. He was rather surprised.

"Who is that?" he asked. "Oh, it is you, Coomaraswamy!"

"That's right."

"Oh, yes, I'm sending my daughter to a school in town. My wife is taking her. They both went to Keerimalai yesterday, bathed in the holy tank and broke coconuts for God Subramanay. All arrangements have been made. They'll be going soon as I have had my morning meal. But tell me, Coomaraswamy, how did you know of it?"

"Well, the whole village is talking about it!"

"Yes, Coomaraswamy," said the headman, "I'm sending my daughter to receive a modern education and learn modern ways for a short time."

"But she's of marriageable age, Ramaswamy."

"I know that," said the father, that's why I am sending her to an English school. You know what young men want these days. You see, Coomaraswamy, I want to get her a young man with a good job, and not a useless fellow who stands in the marketplace with a cigarette in his mouth."

"Perhaps you're right, but I thought you had a nephew in Malaya who would marry your daughter for the asking."

"That's true," replied Ramaswamy, proudly, "I have my nephew in mind; but he has been away for many years and has got beyond my control, but he will not dare refuse if, in addition to being my daughter, Parvati has also a modern education. I suppose you realise my nephew is an engineer in Malaya."

Mrs. Ramaswamy, all this time, had been peeping out of the kitchen, listening to the men's talk. She was happy when they referred to her daughter's marriage. But she did not approve of her husband's nephew. Their talk began to irritate her and she turned to her duties in the kitchen.

As soon as Coomaraswamy had gone, the headman called his wife and asked her if everything was ready.

"Yes," said Mrs. Ramaswamy, "as soon as you've had your morning meal, Parvati and I will have a bite and then we'll be ready to start. But I really don't know how I'm going to pass my days without her."

"Don't exaggerate things. You'll only frighten the girl. She'll be coming home for the holidays, and I've told you many times we are sending her only for a very short time. If you are interested in your daughter's welfare, you shouldn't create difficulties by your foolish behaviour. You know what young men these days want. I mean respectable, educated young men."

"I shan't be foolish," Mrs. Ramaswamy promised, drying her tears.

❊ ❊ ❊

Mrs. Ramaswamy and Parvati had breakfast, gave the final touches to their packing, and asked the carter to get ready.

"All right, Mother," said Subbu, "my 'chariot' will be on the lane before you count ten."

The bullocks had some difficulty in pulling the cart and its occupants through the sandy lanes. The carter had to get down on occasions and help them by pushing the cart by its spokes. But, once the lanes were crossed, they raised their heads and galloped.

They drove in silence for quite a distance until Mrs. Ramaswamy saw a bunch of bananas at a wayside market.

"Stop, Subbu, turn the cart! Let us buy that bunch of bananas and keep it. On the way home, I should like to call on the Temple Road Rasamma. Her youngest brother, I hear, is a fine boy. He is a student in the Colombo University. I should like to give Rasamma a small present and be in her good books. She and her husband are like mother and father to the boy, since his parents died some years ago."

"What about your husband's nephew," asked Subbu, mischievously.

"Don't talk rubbish, Subbu! Turn the cart round!"

Mrs. Ramaswamy elaborated to Subbu on the, virtues of Rasamma's brother until they reached the suburbs of the town. The bullocks put out their tongues and wetted their mouths as they got onto the main street of Jaffna.

"Tamarind School! Go to the Tamarind School!" shouted Subbu, as he beat the bullocks' backs with the reins.

The cart stopped outside the school. Mrs. Ramaswamy got down first and adjusted her sari.

※ ※ ※

The lady Principal rose to receive the visitors. When she saw Parvati, she smiled and patted her cheeks, and then asked them to sit down.

"How old is she?"

"Fifteen."

"Have you brought her birth-certificate?"

Mrs. Ramaswamy shook her head, apologised and said that she did not know a birth-certificate was necessary.

The Principal explained to the visitors that it was customary for the school to keep in its files the birth-certificate or the baptismal certificate of every pupil.

"As soon as I go home, I'll send for the astrologer and ask him to give me a birth-certificate for Parvati," said Mrs. Ramaswamy.

The lady Principal smiled. The matron now entered the office.

"This is our matron," said the Principal, "she'll take good care of Parvati. The girls are all fond of her and call her Akka or Matron Akka."

The matron smoothed the girl's hair. "You come with me," she said to the visitors, "Miss Robinson has to take the English lesson for the Senior Cambridge Class in a short while. I'll do everything for you."

Copious tears were shed before the visitors took leave of each other. The mother kissed her daughter on her cheeks. The matron, knowing by experience that if she interfered the crying would be prolonged, turned her face away. She accompanied them to the door, but kept a few paces behind to give the mother a chance to impart her final confidences.

"Subbu," said Mrs. Ramaswamy, "don't drive the bullocks home. I have just remembered my old friend, Thangamma, wife of advocate Sivalingam. They live somewhere in this town; let us find out where and visit them."

Subbu pulled the reins. The bullocks reluctantly turned their heads.

"Turn the beasts, Subbu, turn the wretches and let us make enquiries."

The carter twisted the tails of the bullocks and kicked one of them. The cart turned and Subbu soon located the advocate's residence and drove into the compound. Thangamma peeped out of the window and recognised her old friend, Sellachi.

"Oh, Sellachi!"

"Oh, Thangamma!"

"Come, sister, come in and tell me everything."

Mrs. Ramaswamy told her friend the reason for her visit to the town.

"Ah!" said Thangamma, "I now understand my husband's repeated remark. "Things are changing rapidly. Coming all the way from Atchuvely, for learning- this would not have happened some years ago."

"We are sending Parvati to the Tamarind School for a short time so that she may learn modern ways and become eligible for an educated young man."

"I guessed that," replied her friend, "but how old is your daughter?"

"Fifteen."

"Well, well, there is plenty of time to think of her marriage," said Mrs. Sivalingam. My husband's niece is sixteen and she is still a student at Tamarind. Advocate Singarayan's daughter, Sunderammal, is twenty and is in the Colombo University reading for her B.A."

"What are you saying, Thangamma? You sound so strange to me. It's already two years since Parvati became a 'big girl'..."

Mrs. Sivalingam noticed that her friend did not approve of her views and was losing her temper. She excused herself and went to prepare lunch.

❋ ❋ ❋

"I want to ask your advice about something," said Mrs. Ramaswamy, lifting her face from the plate of rice and curry. "You'll give me the right advice, won't you, Sister?"

"Of course, Sellachi! Since you're my best friend, I'm naturally interested in your daughter's welfare."

"You see, Thangamma, my husband has one boy in mind and I another."

"Tell me about them."

Mrs. Ramaswamy told her friend about her husband's nephew. And Thangamma noticed that her friend's eyes were getting wet.

"Don't worry, sister," she said, "we women work in subtle ways. Our husbands think that they decide everything. It's not true, sister. They only carry out our plans. They talk, we act. You must work subtly. Don't be a silly woman. I'm sure you're going to win in the end. Now, this very minute, you are going to win! You have won! This is your day, Sellachi!"

Mrs. Sivalingam clapped her hands, rose from her seat, helped Mrs. Ramaswamy to get up, and said, "Now, Sister, whom do you want for your son-in-law?"

Mrs. Ramaswamy's face lit up. "Do you remember Rasamma, our class-mate?"

"Yes, of course!"

"I would like her brother, Krishnamurti, as my son-in-law. He's is a fine boy, young and good-looking. He's a student in the Colombo University and doing well in his studies. I'm sure he'll get a good job. Now, what do you think of my choice?"

"Splendid!" replied Thangamma. "A very suitable match, indeed!"

"Do you think my wish will be fulfilled?" Mrs. Ramaswamy asked, pathetically.

"Of course!" reassured Mrs. Sivalingam. "You must fight your husband unceasingly in this matter. You'll win in the end. Remember, sister, we wives always win."

❈ ❈ ❈

It was fairly late when Mrs. Ramaswamy and Subbu reached Atchuvely. Mrs. Ramaswamy peeped out of the cart and looked for the peasants returning home after their work in the fields.

"Subbu, I don't see any peasants. It must be quite late. Do hurry, Subbu, your master will be waiting for us. We'll have to get back and cook his dinner."

When they reached home, Mrs. Ramaswamy searched for her husband in the house and in the compound, but could not find him. She shouted for him, but there was no answer.

"Subbu, your master is not here. Where can he be?"

"Don't get excited, mother. Probably, he's at Coomaraswamy's. He'll be back soon, don't get worried."

"Sellachi! Sellachi!" somebody called from the front of the house.

Mrs. Ramaswamy rushed out of the kitchen and, to her amazement, saw Rasamma and her husband. The horse-carriage in which they had come was waiting outside. Mrs. Ramaswamy shyly arranged her sari and greeted the visitors. When she had got over her surprise, they exchanged formal questions, and then the visitors broached the subject of their call.

"We were glad to hear you were taking your daughter to Tamarind today," Rasamma said.

"I've just come back from town," Mrs. Ramaswamy said.

"I'm sure Parvati will grow into a fine woman," Rasamma commented.

Her husband nodded.

"She's very beautiful, Sellachi."

"Oh, yes!" the husband agreed.

"I must ask your pardon for something, Sellachi."

"What for, Rasamma?"

"I'm sorry I didn't pay you a visit when your daughter became a 'big girl'."

"Oh, don't be a fool Rasamma!"

Mrs. Ramaswamy excused herself, went to the kitchen and quickly prepared coffee for them. She also brought them betel and arecanut on a silver tray. When they had drunk the coffee, Rasamma's husband again took up the matter. Rasamma took the cue and followed him up more effectively.

"Our dhobi, who is your dhobi as well, has approached us on a certain matter."

"What is it?" asked Mrs. Ramaswamy, knowing dhobis acted as matchmakers.

"Kanthan, our dhobi," continued Rasamma, "spoke highly of your daughter, and he made us a proposal of marriage between Parvati and my brother, Krishnamurti."

"Well," said Mrs. Ramaswamy, placing her hand on her bosom. "All I can say is that it has been my constant wish for a long time, and, since Parvati became a 'big girl', I've been praying for such a union."

"And is that the headman's wish, too?" the man enquired.

Mrs. Ramaswamy nodded.

"The position is this," said Rasamma, "the proposal has come from you through Kanthan. We've thought over the matter and compared the horoscopes of the two. We think it's a suitable match for Krishna."

Mrs. Ramaswamy clapped her hands for joy, then she bit her nails like a child.

"There's happier news yet to come," the man said.

"Let me hear it," said his hostess.

"You tell her," the man said, looking at his wife.

"You see, Sellachi, Krishna has passed his final examination brilliantly and the Government is sending him to England on a scholarship. He intends to become a barrister."

"We're anxious that he should be engaged to a nice girl before he sails for England."

❋ ❋ ❋

Her husband's friend, Coomaraswamy, now came in, looking very agitated.

"What's the matter?" said Mrs. Ramaswamy.

"Well, when the headman came back home this evening and was waiting for your return, the postman brought him a letter which had a Malayan stamp on it."

"Evidently, it was from his nephew," Mrs. Ramaswamy said.

"That's right, it was from his nephew. The headman expected to have good news and he joyfully opened it, but to his great surprise, he found that his ungrateful nephew had written to inform him of his engagement to another girl. He had agreed to marry Broker Sunderam's daughter."

Coomaraswamy, who had expected to hear a good deal from Mrs. Ramaswamy in reply, was surprised to find that she had little to say.

"*Ennay*, are you there?" the voice of the headman came automatically as the outer gate creaked. Mrs. Ramaswamy ran out to greet her husband.

"Oh, you're back!" he said.

"A long while ago," she replied. 'I've been worried about you."

"I'd have come earlier, but I was consulting an astrologer about Parvati's future. He has consoled me. I suppose Coomaraswamy has told you everything. You should never go out of your way to be decent to people ..."

"*Ennay*," the headman went on, "I think it's all for our good. The astrologer says that my nephew's horoscope and Parvati's don't match. The soothsayer also said that Parvati had a brilliant future before her and that she would marry a young man with a good job, good looks and a fine disposition."

"I know somebody who fulfils all those requirements," interposed Mrs. Ramaswamy, courageously.

"Who?"

"Rasamma's brother, Krishnamurti."

"Let me think," replied her husband. "Oh, yes, I remember now. You mean Temple Road Rasamma."

"That's right."

"That's grand!" said the headman. "They are good people, good caste. We must keep them in mind, gradually work up our case. You certainly have ideas …"

DANGER

WHEN his father told him that I was a story-writer he was eager that I should write a story about him. I was flattered by this, yet it touched me. A few years back a smart, sophisticated young woman in London had made a similar request. That, of course, had tickled my vanity.

But though I have not nursed any regrets for never fulfilling the lady's wish, the little boy's repeated requests weighed on my mind.

I had somehow to make a start. "What's your name?" I asked the lad.

"Veeran," he said, "but all my friends call me Danger."

"That's interesting," I said, "because your real name and your nickname mean nearly the same thing."

"My friends must have known that," he commented.

"Anyhow, why do they call you Danger?" I inquired.

"Because I am a dangerous type," he replied. "When I left Malaya my 'classmates gave a big party because they were glad to get rid of me. They were happy I was going."

Then suddenly Danger pulled out a toy gun and pointed it at my chest.

"Will you write a story about me?" he yelled.

I stepped back in panic. I am terrified of guns, even of harmless ones.

"Put that pistol back!" I cried. Danger slid the weapon into his trouser-pocket and laughed.

"Will you write a story about me?" he asked again, his hand returning to his pocket.

"I certainly will," I said. "But don't bring out that dangerous weapon again."

"I won't," Danger replied, "if you'll soon finish the story. I want a story about me. I want my friends to read it. I want the whole world to know about me."

Some weeks after the gun episode, I saw Danger standing outside a jeweller's shop.

"What are you doing here?" I asked.

"Daddy and mummy are, inside," he said. "They're buying jewellery for Rita. You know, Uncle, she's going to get married."

"When?"

"Soon. I hope she marries a bandit."

"Why a bandit?"

"Oh, Uncle, then I can shoot him and carry away all Rita's jewellery. I've shot several bandits in Malaya."

The church was tightly packed with well-wishers and friends on the hot and stuffy afternoon when the marriage of Rita, Danger's elder sister, was solemnized. I preferred to stand outside, under the shade of a Margosa, tree, and fan myself with the nuptial hymn sheet.

Suddenly and mysteriously, Danger popped up from somewhere and beckoned me to bend down to his height.

"He's a bandit all right," he whispered in my ear. "I'm following them to Honeymoon to shoot him. Will you come with me, Uncle?"

"Honeymoon- what do you know about that?" I asked, surprised.

"I know all about it," he said. "That's the place people go to after they marry. Have you written the story, Uncle?"

"No," I replied, "but I'm still working it out in my mind."

"Some writer you are!" Danger said.

Then I saw his hand sliding into his trouser-pocket. I stopped fanning myself and somehow edged my way into the chapel.

A few months after his daughter's wedding, Danger's father, my cousin, came to see me. His chief concern now was for his son and he wanted me to find him a place in one of the over-crowded local educational institutions. Since I had influence at the Tamarind School, my cousin was keen that I should employ it for the benefit of his son.

And so, one fine morning, accompanied by Danger and his certificates, I entered the office of Miss Porter, the Principal of the Tamarind School. Miss Porter could not possibly refuse me and soon led us to the primary department. The lower school was at the time attending morning service, but on seeing Danger the whole assembly fled into the adjoining compound. Both Miss Porter and I were puzzled. Neither of us saw Danger doing anything mischievous.

Soon, however, with Danger firing at the tiny girls and the little boys making feeble efforts to pelt stones at him, the field was turned into a veritable battle ground. The Principal made every effort to get her pupils back to the hall, but the Tamarinders yelled with one voice: "We won't come back till he goes away."

Miss Porter, Danger and I went back to her office.

"I'm afraid I can't admit your protegé," Miss Porter said to me.

Danger stood up and said, "I can speak English, Malay and Chinese."

"Please go away," the Principal admonished the little boy.

On our way back home, Danger gently pressed my hand, saying: "Now you can write a good story about me. You always said there was nothing to write about. What do you say now, Uncle?"

It did not take long for the townsfolk to spread the strange story of Danger and his gun, and no school in Jaffna was ready to enrol him. I was brooding over my failure one day, when my cousin called with his family.

"Never mind, Thamby," he said, patting me on the shoulder. "I'm taking my son back with me to Malaya. I had intended to put him in a good school at Jaffna and settle down here. You know, we exiles have to return to our native land some time. But God has thought fit to postpone that day in my case. It is His will."

Then he gathered his family together and said, "Come, let us pray for Thamby before we wish him good-bye."

Every time he visited me, Danger's father, my cousin Sounderam, prayed for my well-being, especially for the spiritual portion of it. But on this occasion, before we could completely invoke the blessings of the Almighty on me, Danger interrupted him and said: "O God, please help Uncle to become a writer. May Thy mercy be upon him. Amen."

THE MALAYAN PENSIONER

HE came running towards me as I entered The Arcade- a café which serves as a rendezvous for the intelligentsia of Jaffna- his mud-coloured face bursting into a grin, his voice flying before him.

"I was in search of company," he said, grasping my hand, "glad you've come. Let's discuss our experiences. You've travelled in Europe, and I in the Far East. Let's compare notes." He led me to the far end of the café, and we sat close to each other at a small table. The place was rather noisy, with loud conversation and the clatter of cutlery. "People in this country talk too loudly, but we don't. We've travelled far and wide; that's why we're more cultured," he observed.

I summoned the waiter, but he stopped me.

"You mustn't call the waiter. It's his duty to come to you. If he delays, then you can call him. 'If the mountain will not come to Mohammed, Mohammed will go to the mountain.' How do you like that quotation?"

"Excellent," I said, "and most appropriate."

"Where did I get it from? Not from books! You don't have to read if you're a traveller. Travel gathers knowledge. There's only one thing lacking in you. You haven't travelled in the Far East."

"I mean to remedy that soon."

"Splendid. Don't fail to call on me when you are there. I'll give you the time of your life in Bangkok, Kuala Lumpur, Singapore and Penang."

"Thank you."

"You're welcome."

The waiter walked towards us nonchalantly and took down my order indifferently. My friend looked the other way. He resented the attitude of the waiter. However, the meat was tender and palatable, the sautéd potatoes melted on the tongue.

"The Arcade is renowned for its cuisine," I remarked.

"This is nothing." he scoffed at me. "In Malaya I dined on Berkshire pig. A whole pig used to hang in my kitchen."

He told me about satay, a speciality of the Malay kitchen small chunks of meat on coconut stalks, roasted in a spicy sauce over charcoal. Then he described the various Chinese and Bangkovian dishes and convinced me that the Far East was truly a gourmet's paradise. I quickly swallowed some water to wash down the flood of saliva that had gathered in my mouth.

"I'm a Malayan pensioner," he informed me. "I was a surveyor in the Far East- a far-travelling surveyor."

I now felt a kinship with him because of a first cousin I once had in Malaya. He was called Cousin Thampoo. I often recall my childhood impression of him as a kind and generous soul. Whenever he visited Jaffna, he freely distributed China silk to all his relatives.

"One day, when I went to wash my hands," the surveyor drew my attention back to him, "my English boss came after me and said, "Mr. Pillai, I want to see you on urgent business."

""You can't," I told him, "this is my private time." I never had any slavish mentality. I kept the English sahib in his place."

In a world packed with crushing bores it was a great relief to meet a Malayan pensioner, amusing, affable and affluent.

"I suppose you find this place rather dull after your travels abroad," I remarked.

"Dull and dreary," he moaned. "In the Far East, every Saturday night, I went to a cabaret show. What delightful girls! Bangkovian girls with delicate waists and broad hips, Balinese women with luscious breasts and the grace of panthers, and high cheek-boned Malayan lovelies, who give you a slanting look."

Feeling sorry for his bored existence in his retirement, I invited him to a dinner party the next day.

"No, thanks," he said. "Please don't take it amiss. But you can't possibly arrange a party grand enough for me- a man who has wined and dined with Sultans and Tunkus. When a Tunku invited me, I drove in State splendour to his palace. I took my valet with me. He sat beside the chauffeur. My valet wore a uniform, and the initials of my name, S.S.P., were woven into his cap. Several British big guns were guests of the Tunku, and when they spotted my valet, they called him and asked for me, but my valet replied, 'You can't see Master now; Master is being talking to the Sultan of Negri Sembilan and the Raja of Sarawak at the same time; but you can see him in his office tomorrow, if you please'. I showed the British sahib his rightful place. My only weakness is a little superiority complex, never the opposite."

Another Malayan pensioner now entered The Arcade. I invited him to join us. I thought that people who shared the same kind of experience would be eager to meet one another.

"Where have you travelled?" my friend questioned the new-comer.

"I've sojourned in Bangkok, Kuala Lumpur, Singapore and Penang."

"You must have seen only the railway stations!"

"What do you mean?"

"I know," my friend replied. "I knew it at a glance. A man who has really visited those cities would be much more cultured than you."

"Who are you, you insulting bastard?" the new-comer demanded.

"I'm a far-travelling surveyor. Watch your, speech, you brazen-faced fibber."

Before I could intervene in the dispute, my friend had given the visitor a staggering blow under the chin with his clenched fist. The victim toppled over in his chair, banged his head on the cement floor and fractured his skull. He bled. A police inspector soon took charge of the situation.

"Who are you, and why did you cause grievous hurt to this man?" he interrogated.

"I'm S.S. Pillai, a Jaffna Tamil, a Malayan pensioner, a far travelling surveyor, a close associate of Far Eastern Royalty. But this impostor here has seen only the railway stations. He has the impudence to tell me that he, too, has seen all the wonders that I have seen. He's a pathological liar."

"The trouble with you, Mr. Pillai," the inspector said, "is that you have been travelling far too much. It will do you a world of good to stay in one place for a while, preferably a cell. Your new associates will not be Tunkus, but trouble-makers like yourself."

"Don't talk rubbish! A traveller like me will suffer from claustrophobia if confined in a prison-cell."

"I don't quite understand that word."

"How can you? Only travel enlarges one's vocabulary, not a police constable's diary."

"Mind your vocabulary, Mr. Pillai. You're now under arrest," the inspector warned him, "and I'm not a P.C. I'm a police officer. Come!"

He held the surveyor by the arm and forced him forward. S.S. Pillai raised his free hand in Hitler fashion and shouted to me. "So long, my boy, so long! See you in Bangkok, Kuala Lumpur, Singapore and Penang."

The inspector gave him a dig in the back with his baton and said, "See you in jail, you old loafer."

THE INTERPRETER

J.J. a student in a Swabhasa school, attended court one day to give evidence in a family dispute regarding the ownership of a cluster of palmyra trees. In the court he was so impressed by the demeanour of the Interpreter Mudaliar, that he decided to aspire for that post in due course. This meant a switch-over from Swabhasa to English.

But his parents, who were a *Thesawalamai* couple, wished him to continue his studies in his mother-tongue. They felt that their son was making an untraditional move. There was none in their family who was versed in English. However, J.J. recalled to them the impressive costume of the Interpreter Mudaliar. If he were to pass the clerical examination and become an Interpreter Mudaliar, they would have the pleasure of seeing him in an Indian coat, English trousers, shoes of the best quality and Jaffna turban. Besides, there were other advantages such as position, pay and pension. His father nodded agreement. "To the study of Tamil there is no end," he said, "but a knowledge of English brings a job, money and glory."

"Let him go to an English school," his mother said, "If he becomes a government servant, we will be favoured with a piano-playing daughter-in-law."

J.J. was seventeen years old when he embarked on an English education. Since he was already a mature lad he chose the oldest school in Jaffna to help him tide over his difficulties in the quickest time. He showed great eagerness to master the wonderful official language. Whenever anybody asked him why he had set out on this arduous task, he replied: "To the study of Tamil there is no end, brother, but a knowledge of English brings a job, money and glory."

J.J. worked hard at a well-known English Grammar, and he also read the Bible, especially the New Testament, as his missionary tutor had told him that the best English was to be encountered in the Gospels. And after a great effort for many years he succeeded in entering the government clerical service.

J.J. served in different parts of Ceylon in various capacities and finally achieved his life's ambition. He was appointed an Interpreter Mudaliar in a magistrate's court.

It was on a Thursday that Mudaliar J.J. assumed duties. The lawyers had come quite early and had helped the litigants with sound counsel and had helped themselves to their clients' money. The magistrate arrived much later and went straight to his chambers.

The heat of the day was most oppressive. The sun seemed much fiercer here than elsewhere and the black coats of the lawyers circulated the heat evenly over their torsos. The litigants were seated on benches at the far end of the court. Some people stood about listlessly; others squatted on the benches. "Court," called the sergeant as the magistrate took his seat on the Bench. "Attention!"

Everybody rose.

The Interpreter Mudaliar took up the roll. Everyone was eager to see how he would fare on his first day. He handed the calling cases quickly, to the magistrate. Pleas were recorded and dates assigned to everybody's satisfaction. So far so good.

Now and again the court sergeant broke forth: "Less silence."

The proctors laughed at him and exchanged glances. Some made efforts to correct the sergeant but he persisted in shouting, "Less silence!"

A barrister, who was present, appreciated the effectiveness of the sergeant's expression. There was no such thing as absolute nothingness, he said, so 'less silence' was an accurate and scientific description. Besides, 'less silence', which was an original expression, had more literary flavour than 'less noise'. The sergeant bowed to the barrister and shouted louder than before: "Less silence!"

"He's only a Swabhasa sergeant," an inspector of police was heard to remark.

The trials started. The electric fan dispersed hot air, and some hot words passed between the lawyers. A proctor, with a cowlick hair style, was impatient to lead evidence for the prosecution. But the new Mudaliar would not surrender his sovereignty in his own sphere. He felt, rightly or wrongly, that some of the introductory questions should spring from him. He had already asked two questions and had creditably rendered the answers into English.

The witness answered in Tamil. The Interpreter Mudaliar translated the witness's answers into English for the benefit of the Bench and the Bar which had already understood the original.

"What's your profession?" the Mudaliar fired his third preliminary question.

"I sell appam," the witness replied meekly.

The Interpreter hesitated for a moment. Perhaps the English equivalent of bread for appam eluded him momentarily; perhaps he wished to be impressive on his first day in court and his mind was searching for an uncommon word.

However, he was composed enough to remember the advice of the missionary and his mind wandered to the Gospels. And right in front of him he saw a vision. It was

Lord Jesus performing the miracle of the loaves and fishes. "Loaf," the Interpreter thought, "that's the word."

Mudaliar J.J. confidently turned to the court and conveyed the witness' answer: "The witness is a loafer, sir."

The magistrate's normal impassive expression vanished in a split second and he burst into laughter. The lawyers almost simultaneously expressed their mirth. The litigants, quite unaware of the episode, began to giggle as if they had inhaled laughing gas.

"Less silence!" the Swabhasa sergeant yelled.

The court relapsed into its formal and normal dignity. The Interpreter Mudaliar was once again ready to assist the court.

TENNIS

THE doctor and the lawyer started to play. They had two small boys to pick up the balls for them. Their wives sat on the bench in the afternoon sun and watched their husbands, as neither of them wished to play tennis that day.

"Who do you think I saw the other day?" the doctor's wife asked.

"Who?"

"Sita."

"What did she have to say?" the lawyer's wife asked.

"Oh, she bored me talking about her husband. It seems he is now a magistrate and she kept on boasting to me about him. I can't stand women who talk about their husbands all the time."

"Nor can I," the lawyer's wife said. "Some women seem to have nothing else to talk about. Talking about their husbands! Aren't they ashamed of themselves?"

"My husband is winning. Look!" the doctor's wife said.

"Oh, my husband will soon catch up. Wait!" the lawyer's wife said.

"Bole veesu!" the doctor shouted. One of the ball-pickers jumped over a hedge, picked up the runaway ball and threw it to the doctor. The game started again. The lawyer won a point.

"What did I say?" the lawyer's wife asked.

The doctor's wife did not answer.

"Sita is very proud now," she said, "because her husband has been promoted to the bench."

"My husband will soon be a judge," the lawyer's wife said.

The players changed sides and started to play again from different ends of the court. The ball pickers also changed their places.

"I wonder who won?"

"My husband."

"No. My husband."

"Let's ask."

"No, not now. Let them finish."

"Who do you think I went to see the other day?"

"Who?"

"Annamma."

"How is she?"

"She's all right, but I didn't enjoy the visit. She talked about her husband all the time."

"They all seem to do that."

"It's terrible."

"What did she say?"

"She boasted about her husband's practice. It appears he won a case against your husband last week."

"Ha, ha," the lawyer's wife laughed. "Did she say that? Ha, ha."

"She did. She made a big thing of it."

"Ha, ha. I know all about it. My husband told me. He didn't really lose. You see, it was a bad case from the start for my husband. He accepted the brief to please his clients. It was really a victory for my husband. His proctor said so. Everybody present in court thought that."

"It doesn't really matter," the doctor's wife said philosophically, "people lose, people win."

"But it isn't true," the lawyer's wife said angrily.

"I know," the doctor's wife insisted. "The same thing happened to my husband. He performed a difficult operation on a patient whom the D.M.O. had given up as a hopeless case, and when the man recovered the

D.M.O. went about saying that it was all due to his initial treatment. I know it. I know it all so well."

A ball fell near the doctor's wife and the ball picker ran towards it. She kicked the ball. The boy caught it and threw it to the lawyer. He served and his opponent returned it. The lawyer now made a long-arm drive. The ball went past the doctor, sped through a hole in the fence and was temporarily lost. The boy skirted the fence to look for it.

"See? What a neat drive!" the lawyer's wife said. The ball bounced in the tennis court. The game was renewed and the doctor returned his opponent's high stroke with a smash. The ball rose to the height of the fence.

"See? What a smash!" the doctor's wife said.

They were silent for a few minutes and looked at each other. Then they turned to the players. The men played well. They kept the ball up for a long time without missing a single stroke. The women followed the ball, moving their heads from side to side. They soon got tired of it and turned to each other.

"Are you going to the garden party on Saturday?"

"Whose?"

"Leela's."

"Oh, the engineer's wife. I suppose I'll have to go. You see my husband's position demands that we attend such functions."

"Same with us. If one is the wife of a leading lawyer one has certain social responsibilities."

"The garden party is in honour of Leela's husband getting promotion," the doctor's wife said.

"I know," the lawyer's wife said.

"I wonder why he was given promotion."

"For putting up some electrical installations or telephones, I don't know which. But I am told it was a brilliant piece of engineering. Anyhow, you'll hear more about it on Saturday."

"I don't like women who talk about their husbands all the time. I think it's in bad taste. Don't you think so?"

"I agree with you. I think it's in very bad taste."

"Take me, for instance," the lawyer's wife said. "I don't boast about my husband's legal abilities. He gets very difficult cases, but he always wins."

"The same with my husband. He gets very complicated cases, but he is always successful. He's a wonderful surgeon," the doctor's wife replied.

They saw the sun setting on the horizon. There was a crimson glow in the tennis court. The heat had subsided and the wind blew gently.

"I like it here. The breeze is so soothing."

"I'd rather come here than visit those women."

"Look at him. Doesn't he look wonderful in the Chinese silk shirt? I made it for him." the doctor's wife said.

"I've just made a Fuji silk shirt for my husband. He looks marvellous in it, and in this light, oh ..."

The men stopped playing. The ball pickers collected the stray ball and were getting ready to roll the net and undo the tapes. The doctor and the lawyer went to collect their blazers. The women made arrangements to meet for tennis the next day.

THE SCHOLAR

(I)

THE people who were most delighted over Thambirajah's success were his sister Leela and her husband. Leela was much older than her brother, and since the death of his parents many years ago, she and her husband had become Thambirajah's guardians. They had supported him at the university and were now relieved of that burden as Thambirajah's brilliant success in his finals had gained him a scholarship. Soon he would proceed to England to continue his studies on a three years' allowance from the government.

The winning of a scholarship was not an ordinary event in Ceylon. The winner became the chief topic of conversation in family circles and among the educated classes. As Thambirajah cycled in the streets of Colombo in his English drill suit, people pointed to him and referred to him reverently as the government scholar.

The young man himself began to behave differently. He gave up his boyish ways and acted like a man. There was also a noticeable change in his clothes. For instance, they were free from ink stains; and the trousers retained their creases for a longer period.

The news of Thambirajah's success reached all the important towns in the island. In Colombo his friends gave many parties; in Jaffna his sister entertained her friends and relatives to dinner. The guests listened attentively to their hostess's praise of her brother and to the details of his horoscope. They were convinced that the predications of the soothsayers would all come to pass.

Several proposals of marriage were made to Thambirajah, rather they were intended for him, but addressed to his guardians. The proposals came from all directions, at the rate of two a week. Marriage brokers of various types conducted the negotiations. They brought with them photographs and horoscopes of the girls. The dowries promised ran into six figures. Leela and her husband gave serious thought to all the offers and considered them individually.

At first they had intended to wait till their brother returned after completing his studies in England, but now they were nervous he might return with an English wife. They had heard all sorts of stories about the behaviour of European girls. It seemed to them that the girls in the West were only waiting for an opportunity to trap one of the brown denizens of the East. Leela was determined to see her brother married before he left for England.

Thambirajah was given a general idea of the proposals. Whenever his guardians were favourably inclined to one, they discussed it with him. He, however, was absolutely indifferent. The relatives attributed their brother's impassive expression to his shyness. But Thambirajah's mind was far away. There was a girl at the university with whom he was in love.

The girl was called Radha. She was tall, had a slender neck like a swan and walked nonchalantly but gracefully. Thambirajah used to talk to her while waiting in the corridors for the arrival of the professors and had exchanged smiles with her. The whole affair had been a slow process and was distinguished for its mildness. Love at the university was gentle like the evening wind that mildly rustled the leaves of the tamarind tree. Thambirajah had lent his girl friend lecture notes and had written on the margin, "I love you!" Radha had responded by drawing flowers round the words. She had once addressed him as 'Thamby', the familiar shortened form used by his close friends. This was additional proof that she was fond of him. One day, while lending her a book, his little finger had touched her hand and they had both laughed.

Thambirajah gave his sister an inkling of his mind. "Silly boy," she said, "running after girls!" She dismissed the matter with a flourish of her hand. "A girl who flirts at college is not worth considering. She must have a bad character." she said. The love-sick youth went about with a heavy heart. He wrote several letters to Radha, then tore them all up, his courage having failed him at the last moment. He complained to his friends; his moods were extreme and varied. Sometimes he was determined to leave everything to fate; at other times he went about holding his stomach and fainting at frequent intervals. His friends offered two solutions: one, that he should wait as there was a possibility of the various proposals cancelling each other and thus fizzling out, the other, that he should try and elope with Radha. Thambirajah wavered between the two.

Meanwhile, his guardians were making their own plans. The husband and wife did not agree on their choice. There were various points to consider- dowry, caste, looks, the nature and disposition of the parents, from which the character of the girl was inferred, and many other matters. A few days ago Leela had turned down a proposal because the girl, though fulfilling other requirements was too dark. She refused to consider any complexion darker than coffee. That was the limit.

"We must arrange a marriage quickly," she told her husband, "Thamby will be sailing in a few months' time. We must at least get him engaged to a nice girl. The marriage can be consummated on his return." She was restless. "Quick, quick," she said to herself, as she moved about like a wild duck.

(II)

Thambirajah left for Colombo to make the final arrangements before leaving for England. He travelled first class this time, and a servant accompanied him in the third.

The journey from Jaffna to Colombo was long and tedious. The servant got down at some of the stops and brought his master cigarettes, coffee and sweetmeats.

The graduate had brought two books to read on the journey, but he found it difficult to concentrate. He put the book aside and began to think. His mind flitted from one subject to another. For the most part he thought of Radha. But, being a good student, he also gave a few moments to his future in England. Thambirajah was determined to make a success of his post-graduate studies.

"But what about Radha," he said to himself. "Something must be done before I go away."

The scholar now and again peeped out of the window, felt the cool breeze on his face and enjoyed the various sights. The train was passing through different towns and villages. The countryside was green and beautiful and contrasted the luscious growth of the jungle. Once he saw roses and wished he could pluck the prettiest to adorn the lotus dome-shaped bun of Radha.

After attending to the many duties for which he had made the trip to the metropolis, Thambirajah went to the university. He saw a number of his friends in the library. He called a peon and sent a note to Radha in the Ladies' Room. The five minutes seemed like several hours and, at last, instead of Radha, he saw her close friend Rajee. They bowed to each other. Rajee no longer regarded him as an undergraduate. He was a scholarship winner, first in first class, and deserved respect. Thambirajah felt somewhat important. The peons bowed to him at every turn and even the professors now nodded to him differently. The lady students were more liberal with their smiles.

Thambirajah invited Rajee for refreshment in the Tuck shop. They chose a quiet corner before giving the order. He was bewildered at the absence of Radha. "Perhaps she is at a lecture," he said to himself, "But what lecture can it be?" She and Rajee were usually together at this time.

They ordered meat balls and sherbert. A Sinhalese waiter, with a semi-circular comb in his hair served them. The sherbert was of a deep pink colour with ice and *khasa khasa* in it. It refreshed them and acted as an antidote to the intense heat and the chillies in the meat balls.

Everybody looked at them. Some talked of Thambirajah's brilliant academic distinction, others of Rajee's advanced ways. The pair first discussed the professors and their idiosyncrasies; then their respective ambitions. Rajee waited for an opportunity to give him the latest news of Radha. Thambirajah made it easy for her by broaching the subject first.

She told him everything. Radha had been suddenly called back home. Her cousin had returned from England as an F.R.C.S., and her parents, without consulting her, had arranged a marriage between them. The wedding would take place soon. Rajee did not know whether Radha approved of the choice. The last letter from her friend had only mentioned the incident without any comments.

Thambirajah nearly fainted. His knees shook and his mouth went dry. Rajee did her utmost to console him. She missed Radha very much, but his loss was far greater.

They ordered more sherbert and sat for a little while. He explained his position. His love for Radha had been mild in its initial stages, but now it had taken a more serious turn. Since leaving the university he had no thought for anybody but her. It was impossible for him to love anybody else. In his room in Jaffna, he had a photo of some of the students of the university; Radha was in it and morning noon and night he looked at the photo. He also had a painting by a Chinese artist of two swans swimming on a lake. These were the only pictures he possessed and they both reminded him of Radha. "Morning, noon and night," he cried, "I think of her. Oh, what can I do now? I feel so helpless." "Sh, Sh, there are people around us," Rajee said. Thambirajah dried his eyes with a silk handkerchief.

They both decided to get in touch with Radha. Rajee offered to act as intermediary. She wrote the letter; he helped her.

Rajee did not go straight to the subject. As a precautionary measure she put in a few introductory lines about herself and the life around her at college; then she mentioned Thambirajah's plight and suggested an elopement. He would take the necessary step on hearing from her.

The letter reached Radha when she was having tea with her fiancée. Her mother had not opened it as it was addressed in Rajee's handwriting. She approved of the correspondence between the two highly educated lady students.

"This is from Rajee," Radha told her fiancée. I've already told you about her. She is a wonderful girl, my best friend. She writes the most marvellous letters. Rajee! Dear Rajee! What news have you this time? Let us see, shall we? eh! eh!"

She soon realised the mistake she had unwittingly committed. Her fiancée was furious. They were silent for a while and avoided each other's eyes.

Radha at first had been unwilling to marry her cousin. She had not foreseen the event and had been taken unawares when her mother spoke of the wonderful qualities of her husband's nephew and broke the news of the engagement.

Radha had even overcome her modesty and had told her mother of her fondness for Thambirajah. "Who has the money?" her mother had replied. "A university scholar would want a fantastic dowry. Don't make ridiculous suggestions!"

And so her mother, failing to persuade her by sound advice and entreaties, had finally used force.

The father's pressure had been greater. Once, during those days, when Radha was hit by her mother with a broomstick, the father had stood by and said, "There is no temple holier than a mother; there is no mantram to override the words of a father." When Radha still persisted in her devotion to Thambirajah he had shouted, "A virgin should not talk like that."

Thus had the girl given way. She had had to choose between her family and Thambirajah. There had been no way out, as he had seemed to lack all incentive to action. He was a scholar and a dreamer. "You can do what you like," she had finally told her parents. "I leave it all to you."

Radha gradually got accustomed to her fiancée. The couple, being educated and modern, were given the liberty of seeing each other before marriage. The meeting took place in the future bride's house under the supervision of her mother who came into the sitting room at frequent intervals to make sure that they behaved properly. He brought his fiancée presents and pleased her in a hundred ways. She found him interesting and kind and soon accepted heroically the future life planned for her by her parents.

Rajee's letter, therefore, came like a thunderbolt and disturbed the equanimity of the pair. Radha's thoughts were of Thambirajah; her fiancée became uneasy. They tried to ease each other's position. In the end, Radha's state so enraged him that he decided to take action, He showed the letter to her parents and a civil war started. Radha was in tears. The future son-in-law soon restored peace with a solution.

He wrote to the warden of the university hostel where his rival had stayed during his undergraduate days. Rajee's part in the plot was suppressed as a favour to Radha. The warden exercised minor acts of guardianship over the scholar. He informed Thambirajah that a government scholar did not have the same freedom of action as ordinary students and advised him in the interest of his career to refrain from such activities. The warden promised not to bring the matter up before the University Board. Radha's father, who had been raving like a lunatic for some days, referred the matter to Thambirajah's relations.

Leela was surprised at the behaviour of her brother and was furious that he should of his own accord, make plans for his marriage. "It is dangerous," she said, "to let him go to Europe without any attachment at home. He will let us all down." And she set about quickening the negotiations with regard to her brother's matrimony. She abandoned all her house-work, left everything in charge of the servants, and gave all her time to the matter in hand.

(III)

Despite all precautions the story of the Thambirajah-Radha love affair spread all over the university. The sympathies of the undergraduates were with the lovers. Rajee went up in the estimation of the students. "Bold of her to have taken that step," they said, "she is really modern."

Men students vied with one another to be in her good graces. They walked or cycled behind her, with her, and past her. "Hope she practises what she preaches," they said.

Rajee, however, was too busy consoling Thambirajah and devising further means of access to Radha. The scholar could neither eat nor sleep. He seemed to be living entirely on sherbert. One day a telegram reached him. It was from his sister. It said "Take-care of your character. Arrangements made. Letter follows. Leela."

Thambirajah tore the telegram into a thousand bits, threw them into the air and abandoned himself to the winds. He and his hair were blown about in all directions, and when he banged into someone, he said, "Not I, but the wind."

The promised letter soon followed. It began by scolding Thambirajah for his stupid behaviour, then it gradually unfolded details of a marriage proposal. The family concerned were of good caste and resided in Cinnamon Gardens, the Mayfair of Colombo. They were offering Thambirajah a dowry of seventy five thousand rupees in cash and property and jewellery worth another seventy five thousand. The girl was of olive complexion with regular features, intelligent and played the piano. She wore the sari in a hundred different ways with a silver belt. Her jewellery consisted principally of diamonds.

Thambirajah read the letter to Rajee. They both resented it. He made up his mind to go back to Jaffna and cancel the engagement.

"There are other young men who have gone to Europe without being previously married," she said. "Quite so," he replied.

They then discussed other means of contacting Radha. Rajee excused herself early that afternoon as she had to prepare an essay for her tutor. Thambirajah was in great despair and and could not sleep at all that night. He felt a sinking feeling inside him, and seemed to be losing his entire personality. "Radha! Radha!" he cried, "it's all finished ..." A pause and then "No, oh, no, this is not the end. I must find a way, out ... how can I? Oh, Radha!"

(IV)

After a few days, Thambirajah and his servant took the night train to Jaffna. The master wished to be alone and told his servant not to disturb him.

The scholar had a sleeping berth. He was restless and paced up and down the compartment. Hawkers came round at various stops. He bought a packet of cigarettes and smoked them one after another. Later in the night he closed the window, put the shutters down and cut himself off from the rest of the world.

The train reached Jaffna the next morning. The platform was full of people waiting for the arrival of their friends and relatives. Thambirajah's brother-in-law and his intended fatherin-law were there.

Most of the passengers were peeping out of the windows as the train steamed in. They smiled and waved to their relations.

The servant got down and located his master's compartment. The scholar's relatives were surprised to find the shutters down. They opened the door and found Thambirajah lying on his back, with one hand on the bed, the other hanging down limply. "Thambirajah! Thamby!" his brother-in-law called, "this is Jaffna. Get up!" There was no reply.

The railway staff mechanically removed Thambirajah and his suit-case. The doctor discovered a half-eaten apple on the floor. He examined it. "Poisoned apple," he said, "an original method."

Leela fainted when she saw her brother's body. And when she recovered, she cried "Thamby! Thamby! My only brother My brother who was like a son to me, don't leave me behind! Burn me with Thamby! Burn me on the funeral pyre! On the …"

Her husband was left alone to make arrangements for the funeral.

"What a tragedy!" cried the mourners. "He could have got any girl he wanted, yet he killed himself for one."

Leela lay prostrate on the bed, soaking the pillow with her tears. The doctor sent the apple to be analysed. The University Council soon met to appoint a successor to the scholarship.

SOLOMON'S JUSTICE

NORMALLY, I would never have appeared in such a matter. For one thing, I hate to go into a hospital; for another, it pains me to accept fees from a person in mourning. But Ramu insisted that I should do my duty as a barrister and smiled most ingratiatingly. I decided to oblige him.

Ramu's relative was the first wife of the dead man. She and her son had brought him to the hospital in the morning, suffering from a sudden ailment. They had made all arrangements to conduct the funeral rites in their house. But there was an objection, for another woman, too, claimed the body as that of her late husband and, accompanied by her children and a host of relatives, demanded that the corpse be handed over to her. I was briefed to appear for Ramu's relative: wife number one.

I entered the hospital. It was not so forbidding as I had feared. A nursing nun came and greeted me. She was clad in the severe dress of her calling, but smiled soothingly, the smile of her profession. She informed me that the coroner had not yet arrived and that I was to wait for him.

I was shown into a large room. There were two young women, one at work, the other sprawled in a low chair. The latter smiled at me with her eyes, and when I smiled back the same way, she coquettishly dropped them.

"Won't you sit down?" she said. She wore a glittering sari, quite out of place in a hospital, and one got the impression that she was waiting her turn in a mannequin parade. I sat down.

"Are you a film star?" I asked her.

"Don't be ridiculous," she said, brushing aside my remark with a flourish of her jewelled arm. "I am a medical student."

The house officer now came in to announce that the coroner had arrived. He shot a swift glance at the girl before leaving.

"He seems to like you," I remarked as soon as he was out of the room.

She gave me a forlorn look, then glanced at her nails. They were painted a transparent blue and sparkled like Ceylon sapphires. Her soft, coffee-powder complexion had changed into a darker hue and a cloud had descended on her small, Mongoloid face.

Ramu now swept into the room to fetch me to the coroner. She involuntarily rose, dropped her eyes and departed.

The coroner was dressed in white, the appropriate colour for an Asian funeral, and also wore a black necktie, the symbol of European mourning. He recorded the statements of the parties and informed them that he would presently produce them before the magistrate for his advice and recommendation. Then he threw me an enigmatic smile, as if to say that my case was a dubious one.

"I order both parties to keep the Queen's Peace till the magistrate comes," the coroner added.

"The Queen's Peace in Buckingham Palace?" Ramu queried mischievously.

"Look here," the coroner admonished him. "You are supposed to be in mourning today, but you're behaving exactly like a circus clown. Will you all keep the Queen's Peace?"

"We will," replied Ramu, a poignant smile hovering on the corners of his mouth.

The magistrate was an uncommonly tall and hulky person with a perpetual smile on his parted lips. I presented the case for the first woman. She was the wife of the deceased by habit and repute. However, the second woman submitted a certificate of marriage to prove that she had been legally married to the dead man. The magistrate perused the document.

"Here's ample proof that the second woman was the lawful wife," he observed. "I'll have to advise the coroner to hand over the corpse to her."

"My client's marriage to the deceased was by habit and repute," I insisted. "I shall call witnesses to support her claim. Besides, she has made all arrangements to conduct the obsequies in her house."

"If you don't settle the matter peacefully among yourselves, I'll make my own order," the magistrate said, "and wherever the funeral takes place, see that absolute peace is maintained. You are supposed to be mourners, not rioters."

He seemed angry but the inevitable smile soon crept to his face banishing the intruding anger.

But there was uneasiness among both sections. Neither party would give in to the demands of the other. My client, wife number one, mourned ostentatiously, her hair was dishevelled and hung down to her shoulders. Her rival was comparatively calmer though her eyes were red and tear-stained. She took deep breaths and her bosom rose and fell. Ramu moved about canvassing support for his relative. The crowd seemed restless.

My client cried: "I brought my husband to the hospital. Please, give him back to me, sir."

"The other woman wailed: My husband! Oh, my husband! Please hand the father of my children to me, sir."

The crowd now surged forward and approached the magistrate's table. There was an angry demeanour on their faces.

"Move back all of you immediately," the magistrate cautioned them. They withdrew sheepishly.

"The Queen's Peace. Keep the Queen's Peace," the coroner squeaked.

There was a mild stir again when the Mother Superior of the hospital edged her way through the assembly. Addressing His Honour in a voice that was bold and toneless, she sought permission from him to intervene as amicus curiae in the dispute.

"You're most welcome," the magistrate said with a benevolent smile.

"Let us invoke the guidance of the Bible," she prayed. "The Holy Book cites the decision of King Solomon when he was confronted with two women, each of whom claimed to be the mother of the same baby."

The magistrate rose with a sudden abruptness as if his seat were on fire.

"You mean," he asked with a tremor in his voice. "You mean ... cut ... you mean ... cut." And a sad, half-formed smile appeared on his face for a moment, and then flitted away.

LOVELY DAY

"LOVELY day," said Pat, waking me up one summer morning in London. I grunted, turned over on my side and went to sleep again.

"Silly boy," she said, and went into the kitchen. She soon called me for breakfast, saying: "Lovely Day."

I laughed into my coffee. "Is it?" I asked.

"Don't you think so?"

"Perhaps, but it's always lovely where I come from."

"Must you be unpleasant first thing in the morning? It's only a greeting. Why don't you get used to it?"

"What do you want me to say?" I protested.

"Say 'Lovely Day'."

Now it was Pat who laughed into her coffee and spilled it on her dressing-gown. "Don't you ever say 'Lovely Day'?" she asked.

"No."

"What do you say then?"

"Nothing."

"What do you do on a lovely day?"

"Same as on other days. It's always lovely."

Pat giggled and spilled her coffee again. "Go," she said, "go on your rounds."

I looked back at Pat as I went to the bathroom. She was still laughing.

On my way to town, I stopped at a tobacconists' to buy cigarettes. The woman at the counter said: "Lovely Day."

"Yes," I said, "but I want twenty cigarettes."

"You don't seem to believe it," she said, as she handed me the cigarettes and the change.

"I do," I replied. "It's really lovely and warm, but I haven't yet got into the spirit of that greeting."

"Greeting? What do you mean greeting?"

I hurriedly left the shop.

Nobody greeted me at a small cafe where I went for a cup of coffee. I sat near the window, sipped my coffee and looked out. It was really a fine day. The sky was a lovely blue and the people on the pavements looked happy. But before I had finished my coffee it was raining.

The lovely day had suddenly turned into a miserable one. It rained slowly and one felt it was going to be one of those long-drawn-out rainy days. There was a melancholy drone in the air, dirty slush on the ground, and the wind was chilly. It was cold. Everybody looked unhappy.

I covered my head with a newspaper and dashed into Cohens' bookshop in Bloomsbury. It was a strange shop, with a quaint selection of books. I could spend hours looking round. But Cohen always grumbled.

"Bloomsbury is no longer a book centre," he would say. "They all go to Charing Cross Road now. Think of it, isn't it awful, people going to Tottenham Road for books? Once upon a time my boy, Bloomsbury was the place. Still, it has a name, I'd rather sell a good book here than piles of rubbish there. Well, well, we'll see … hi, hi, hi!"

He would chuckle and often give me a slight discount on the marked price of his second-hand books.

I was so engrossed in a book that I didn't notice Cohen coming out of his office and peeping over my shoulder to look at the book I was reading.

"Good book, my boy," Cohen said.

"Oh, hello, Cohen," I said, "Lovely Day."

"Lovely Day?" Cohen shouted. "It's a horrible day! Simply awful! Look at that dreary rain. Ordinarily I don't get many customers here, and when it rains like this …" he threw up his hands in despair.

"Look at me," he said, pointing to his feet. "It was fine this morning and so I wore a pair of sandals. Now it's cold and my feet are frozen. Lovely day, eh, eh?"

"Don't take it to heart," I pacified him, "It was only a greeting."

"Greeting? What a greeting on a day like this!"

I thought it wise to leave Cohen to brood over his misfortunes alone, so I went to lunch. The Indian restaurant was empty, except for an American soldier in a corner who was eating curry and rice with only a fork. A gloomy little waiter welcomed me and showed me to another corner. I asked for the manager and was told he was asleep.

"He has been sleeping all morning Sir," the waiter informed me. "Business bad, very bad."

My food was served with unusual alacrity. As I ate, the waiter stood at a distance and looked vaguely at the soldier, who was making rude remarks to himself about the food.

"Drunk," the waiter whispered to me as he passed. "He's drunk."

The manager now appeared, rubbing his hands together, a picturesque figure in his turban, long-coat and tight trousers. He made a generous bow to his two customers.

"All right, sir?"

"Yes," I said, "delicious curry."

"We always give the best menu, sir," he said. Then he went up to the soldier and, rubbing his hands together, said: "Lovely day, sir."

"You bloody fool!" the soldier yelled, "look outside. It's a lousy day!" He pushed the manager forcibly. The waiter intervened and pathetically said: "He has been sleeping all day, sir."

"Sorry, chum," the soldier said, "and don't wear these tights again. I'd certainly like to see an American glamour girl in tights, but not your skinny, bandy legs."

The manager, hurt, crossed and stood near me, rubbing his hands, as if nothing had happened. Then he bent over me and whispered: "I only wanted to be nice. You know, sir, I'm always nice to my customers. 'Lovely day' is only a greeting. Was I wrong, sir?"

"No," I soothed him, it's only a greeting." The rain poured down the windows of the restaurant.

A few minutes later, I stepped into the street. The sun was shining, the sky was clear and blue again, and it was warm. An old friend was hurrying towards me.

"Don't tell me," I forestalled him, as he approached. "I know. It's a lovely day!"